PLANE TREE DRIVE

PLANE TREE DRIVE

LYNETTE WASHINGTON

MidnightSun

First published 2017 by MidnightSun Publishing Pty Ltd
PO Box 3647, Rundle Mall, SA 5000, Australia.
www.midnightsunpublishing.com

Cataloguing-in-Publication entry is available from the
National Library of Australia.
http://catalogue.nla.gov.au

Cover design by Kim Lock
Cover art by Joanne Knott
Internal design by Zena Shapter

Printed and bound in Australia by Griffin Press. The papers used by MidnightSun
in the manufacture of this book are natural, recyclable products made from wood
grown in sustainable plantation forests.

'Yet high over the city our line of yellow windows must have contributed their share of human secrecy to the casual watcher in the darkening streets, and I was him too, looking up and wondering. I was within and without, simultaneously enchanted and repelled by the inexhaustible variety of life.'

The Great Gatsby
F. Scott Fitzgerald

For my family and friends, who are everything

THE MOST IMPORTANT PEOPLE

Maurice Muso, father of Amily, Jacqui's husband, founder of The Shed Dogs

Jacqui Maurice's wife, mother of Amily

Amily Maurice's estranged teenage daughter

Aria Friends with Suzie, has a fling with Tim

Tim Singer/songwriter, womaniser, addict and father of Annabelle and Jacob, Alice's ex, no fixed address

Suzie Friends with Aria, marrying Joaquin, lives in the same apartment block as Faraj

Jennifer Filmmaker, married to Dan, mother of Ava, Alexander's childhood sweetheart

Dan Married to Jennifer, father of Ava

Ava 18-month-old daughter of Jennifer and Dan

Alexander Childhood sweetheart and unrequited love of Jennifer

Hunni Department store worker, friend of hermit crabs

Poppy Teenager with a nosy brother

Lia Has an open marriage with Amos

Amos Has an open marriage with Lia

Pete Long-term friend of Lia

Riley and Ethan Lia and Amos' children

Donna — Dating Damien, owns a dog called Jesus

Damien — Dating Donna

Jimmy — Part-time community radio host, part-time porn-watcher

Andy — Jimmy's mysterious co-host

Alice — Tim's ex, mother of Annabelle and Jacob, dating Sundance

Annabelle and Jacob — Tim and Alice's teenage children

Sundance — Ponytail-sporting hippie, dating Alice

Faraj — Young Afghani asylum seeker with no fixed address

Coralie — Housing officer who is managing Faraj's case

Ruby — Travel agent, the woman Faraj meets on the train

Kerry — Teenage Alexander's girlfriend

Colette, Mike and Simon — Jennifer and Alexander's childhood friends

Stevo — Martha's travel agent

Leyton — Demolition site manager at The Theatre

Florence — Elderly wife of Doug

Doug — Trumpet player, Florence's husband

Eldon — Florence and Doug's adult son

Gloria — Florence's friend

Neville — Gloria's husband

Brock	Painter on retreat with Jennifer
Bruce	Grumpy middle-aged gambler
Hal	Lonely old man with a roof in need of repair
Gladys	Jennifer's confidant at her PTSD Support Group
Scarlett	Owner of the 'shed for sale'
Marg	Woman who talks to animals
Denise	Owner of Jeremiah the cat, Marg's neighbour
Martha	Charles' wife, adventure seeker
Charles	Martha's husband
Gary	Married to the late Molly, father of Sarah, works in the carpark
Sarah	Daughter of Gary and Molly, fond of her Oma, fruitcake and flowcharts
Abdul	Works with Gary in the carpark
Stella	Graham's wife
Graham	Stella's husband, on a brave quest
Dalton, Rowena, David and Miranda	The Shed Dogs

MAURICE, JACQUI AND AMILY

Secrets and Plane Trees

Jacqui hated the house on Plane Tree Drive. She moved in with me because she was pregnant with Amily. But the trees' bark peeled in flaky patches that used to make her frown and scratch. Old and high-branching, their elaborate forked leaves were phosphorescently green in summer, camp orange in autumn and then absent in winter. In spring, they scattered fibrous pollen. There wasn't a season she liked or even tolerated. She used to look up at the branches, reaching over the road towards each other, and mutter under her breath, 'monstrous' or, 'it'll be the death of me'. She said the trees made her feel like she was in prison. She was convinced the street was shadowy, secretive. Something about the gnarled fingers of the branches especially made her skin crawl. Of course, it was nothing to do with the trees at all.

We were in the middle of the street, in a dreadfully boring cream brick family home. To the east were the flats and subsidised housing and to the west, the old stone cottages that had been extended and renovated into ostentatious upper-middle class homes. It was comfortable, a place I enjoyed coming back to. But we were the in between and we never did quite make it work.

TIM, ARIA AND SUZIE

How to Disappear Incompletely

So we're on the tram and it's 9am and standing room only. Tim's arm is raised to hold the leather strap so that he doesn't stagger and he's wearing last night's black tank top and I can see his armpit hair, the pale underside of his skinny arm, and his ribs poking through translucent skin. Pale blue veins run undisturbed by scars, parallel to his bones. Seemed so rock'n'roll a few hours ago.

I'm trying to be polite, travelling back to the city with him, and he's tracing the tattoo on my forearm. Fingertips on my ink. Way too intimate, man. I flinch and he looks up, mascaraed black semi-circles under bloodshot eyes. Those eyes say, 'after what we did last night?' and I look out the window and tuck my arm away.

'So I don't think I can come to the gig tonight,' I say to the blue sky outside.

'That's cool. Come by after? I'll get you a plus one for the after-party.'

'It's just that I've got this thing on and I don't know when it will finish,' I say.

'Aria, babe, just come, we had a good time last night, didn't we?'

I can't figure out a way to say it nicely and there's a glint of despair hiding under his casual tone.

'Alright, I'll try.'

The eavesdropping commuters on the tram all know I'm lying. When we get off and I point to his hotel it will be the last time I see him. Except maybe on *Rage*.

The tram slides into the city square and people spill off in a swarm. We – in last night's clothes, bed-hair, pale skin and tattoos – let them pass in a puff of aftershave and perfume.

'Coffee?' he says.

He'll be leaving town tomorrow. It's just coffee. And I need coffee.

'Okay.'

We head to the markets where I know a great little café. Old wire seats with paint scratched off by anxious fingernails and pink Formica-topped tables that wobble with nerves. It's as if the furniture itself is caffeinated. But the coffee's good.

He buys me a short black double shot and we sit at our fretful table. We hold our cups with two hands and take our first hot sip simultaneously. Strange, awkward symmetry. Then a fleeting moment when I see a shadow skittering across the floor – a rat? No, it's too big, but I follow the shape and find nothing there – a shadow that has no solid form.

The coffee makes its way down my throat. My chest constricts and my heart thumps, a racehorse is galloping its way down my oesophagus wearing hot iron shoes. I put my hand to my throat, and he's doing the same thing.

'Strong coffee...' I say. But I've sucked down Turkish short blacks like they were air and never had this happen.

'Do you feel it in your throat?' he asks.

I nod. 'And my stomach. It's moving down.'

He puts his hands over his ears like a comic book character blocking out a painful sound.

'Mine's going up. What the fuck?' he says too loudly and people eyeball us then go back to their coffees.

I grab his hand and we run, lock ourselves into the disabled cubicle and stare at each other.

'What the hell kinda coffee was that?'

I look down at the place where I feel the warm liquid, slower now, like it's settled in my belly. Lifting my Dead Kennedys t-shirt, I expect to find all sorts of nothing strange, but instead I can see a giant gaping hole where my gut used to be.

'Hell...' he says and reaches his hand out and pushes it through me. His arm is a warm breeze.

'Sweet Jesus!' I yell. But it doesn't hurt.

He pulls up his sweat-stained tank top to show me his stomach. It's all there, it's not happening to him and that makes it worse. But then I look up and there is a hole there now, where his face used to be. Like that rat-shadow: something, then nothing. No more black-ringed eyes, stained teeth and stubble. All I can see is his hair; his trademark black fop which used to cover an eye now looks like a curtain opening onto an empty stage. I lift my hand up to see if I can push it through his face and he shrieks.

'No! Don't do it!'

He has no mouth. Where is his voice coming from? The sound of it resonates inside my skull. I don't stop anyway and my hand goes all the way through, and I can feel a sort of throbbing inside his skull and I hear – or maybe feel – his sharp intake of breath as my hand goes all the way to the wall behind him. His breath flows over my fist before it gets to his lungs, which seems *romantic* and makes me think of my heart. Is it still beating in there under the Kennedys?

Pulling my t-shirt down from the collar, I don't know what I want to find, but I have to know what's there. I see my bra and my cleavage moving up and down too fast, I'm gasping like a smoker on a treadmill. There is no hole there, my heart is intact. My gut might be blasted away, and his brains may be blown out, but my heart is there. Maybe that's why this somehow feels like falling in love. Is this how Suzie feels? Is that why she's doing it?

Everything's Turning to White

In my white dress, I am a ghost. Pale skin, blonde hair, white silk-covered shoulders. Invisible, without even putting on the veil. Imagine that.

Aria is white too, but hers is the kind of white that comes from living nocturnally. Her tatts poke angrily out of the emerald green satin dress that she would never choose to wear but accepted with a smile out of sheer friendship.

Across town the church is decorated with large ribbons of white, the same fabric as my dress. There are white roses in bouquets on the pews. I am holding a small posy of white daisies. I painted my nails nude, but there isn't much pink there – it looks white to me.

'Oh, Suzie you look divine,' Aria says.

She is inspecting me, fussing. Dress gets smoothed, hair gets smoothed, cheeks get smoothed. Veil is puffed over my back like a billowing benevolent cloud.

I try to smile at Aria.

'This is the happiest day of my life,' I say, trying not to cry.

'Suzie, you're daft. You're not letting yourself enjoy this. You don't know how to be happy.'

She is wrong. I do. I did.

She reapplies my lipstick for the fifteenth time this hour and pronounces me ready.

'But we can't go yet. You have to be late.'

This is the final straw. These stupid traditions, absurd rules about how to be a bride. I am setting myself up for a life of unlivable rules, beginning now. For Aria, life is *lived* late, so much so that it's the norm. Late nights. Late mornings. Late texts. Late periods.

I pick up my train, my ridiculous train that my mother talked me into, and walk out the door.

'Suze! What the hell are you doing?'

I climb the stairs to Joaquin's apartment on the floor above. I knock loudly on his door.

I can hear Aria running after me, struggling to make it up the stairs in her stupid satin fishtail gown.

I knock again.

'He's at the church already, Suz,' Aria says.

Of course he is. He's never late for anything.

I want to sit down but the corridor floor is filthy and it will ruin my dress. I am enough of a bride to stop myself from doing *that* at least. I lean against Joaquin's door. Footsteps come from the floor below and my heartbeat stops. Maybe he changed his mind and is coming back?

No, it's only the boy who lives on and off in the flat above. I smile at him. His head is down, looking at his shoes, where the blinding whiteness of my ludicrous dress draws his eyes. They trace the white up up up to my face and he looks at me with his empty brown eyes and I can tell that he's hardly seeing me.

'Hi Faraj,' I say.

He nods and keeps walking up to number 6.

For a mad moment I consider asking him what's wrong – just to delay what I really have to do.

Aria takes my hands and draws me back into the moment.

'Suze, shall we head off to the church now?'

'I thought you said we had to be late?'

'Better early than never.'

She's panicking. Her job is to get the bride to the church and she knows I'm on the verge. She can see herself walking up the aisle – alone – delivering a message to the hapless groom. The scene plays out in my mind, complete with silent, dry weeping from Joaquin and wet, messy hysterics from my mum. I let my imagination continue to play out the scenario. I go home to Plane Tree Drive. Joaquin and I stop looking for a bigger place to share. I come home from work at night to sit in front of the telly with wine and microwaved food. I avoid Joaquin in the corridor.

Any way I look at my life, it's a cliché.

Raised voices sink down from number 6 and Faraj comes back down the stairs. This time he stops and speaks. Slowly, thinking through each word.

'Today you marry Joaquin?'

I hesitate before I answer, 'Yes.'

'He is your home now. You always have someone, Suzie.' Faraj says.

Joaquin is my home. I suppose it's true.

I want to hug Faraj, but he looks like he would break if I touched him.

'Yes,' I say.

Faraj nods and walks down the steps.

JENNIFER AND AVA

Smoke and Broccoli

The lean-to sunroom is small but bright. I've finally managed to put brush strokes on the canvas, but they are infantile and amateurish, broad and clumsy. It's yet another horizon, an open sweeping vista in the pastel light of dusk. I never paint people, houses or streets. Never trees with crooked fingers leaning over each other, grasping and locking themselves together.

After an hour or so I wash out the brushes, skol a cold cup of tea, then scrub mould from the toilet bowl. These jobs leave a more indelible imprint than anything on canvas or paper. The steam from the kettle creates a soon-to-be pus-filled scorch on my wrist, the skin in the valleys between my fingers cracks inside my rubber gloves, my back aches from bending over the bowl. All these things are real and deep. No matter how much colour I layer onto the canvas, it remains shallow and detached.

As I peel off the rubber gloves, Ava cries and the idea that I was allowing to fester in my mind as I scrubbed the toilet bowl – the idea of a different life – is smoke. Gone, in the face of immediate demand.

I pop a rusk in her mouth and pile her into the car. We drive to the local supermarket, her satisfaction with the slimy breadstick waning with each intersection.

My hopes of a quick trip to the veggie isle are thwarted when she spies the bright plastic toys on a spinner. Her hunger is forgotten for a while, replaced by a bigger need – an oversized pink bubble wand. I park her pram in front of the spinner, stomp on the brakes and race to the next isle, grab broccoli, potatoes and carrots and race back to her.

My heart is thumping.

I shouldn't have left her there, even for a moment. I shouldn't. I shouldn't. I shouldn't.

I let her take the bubble wand because of the guilt and I can't deal with a tantrum right now.

Back home, dinner eaten, bath taken, the bed routine hangs over me like a railway sleeper, waiting to crush me for any mistake or omission. I can't miss a step, every movement is critical to ensure a good night's sleep.

Finally, she's down.

'How was your day?' Dan asks as he makes himself a toasted sandwich for dinner.

I shrug. 'Same old, same old.' But I'm thinking about scrubbing the toilet bowl, imagining something else. I shut my eyes and am haunted again by Alexander, his eyes like secrets his face is trying to hide.

'I'm going to bed,' I say. 'Didn't get much sleep last night.'

'Hopefully she sleeps through tonight. I'll just watch some telly for a while.' Dan kisses me on the forehead and settles down with his dinner in front of the TV.

In bed, I switch on the electric blanket and curl up. In these quiet moments my thoughts roam free, uncensored. Of course Alexander is there. I try to remember his smell, but can't. It's been too long, and the bed smells like Dan. He didn't wait for me, he went on and lived his life.

What will I will tell Ava, when she's older and thinking about these things? If she falls in love and is too scared to say it out loud, what will I say to her? The answer comes immediately, impulsively, without argument or interrogation. It's so simple. I'd say to her, 'Tell him.'

One am and Ava cries. Adrenalin jolts me awake and I'm staggering to her room before I'm fully conscious, and before Dan has even registered what is going on.

I know one thing for certain: there is no separation of her and me. I can't find a boundary between us. I don't know where she ends and I begin. I could drown in her and I realise if I do, I'm one step further from him.

MAURICE AND JACQUI

He Said/She Said

Jacqui: This conversation gouges tracks in my brain. It makes my synapses bleed just to *think* about talking about this again.

Maurice: You and your bloody tracks and synapses. Can't you speak like a normal human being for once?

Jacqui: Okay, here's something you might understand. *Nothing with you ever changes!*

Maurice: I'm an optimist. My glass is always half full.

Jacqui: My eyes are half shut. I'm so bored. Bored with you. Bored with our life, that incidentally was *always about you*. Never me, never Amily. Bored with this argument. I need to sleep now. Tomorrow we will wake up and pick up where we left off. And next week, and next month. We go in circles. Over and over.

Maurice: Maybe *that's* what the celebrant meant...

Jacqui: What? You're mumbling again.

Maurice: The celebrant. When he gave us the rings and said it symbolised the circular nature of love.

Jacqui: He was an idiot. You are an idiot.

Maurice: He was a good man, may he rest in peace.

Jacqui: He was a pervert. But don't worry, he's resting in peace. He got the prime spot on the red velvet club chair. He's eating grapes that were peeled by Botoxed angels. His toenails are being nibbled by grooming mice who have been starved of cheese for this very purpose. His shoulders are being massaged by gnarly fingered deviants who have been released from hell on temporary visas. His –

Maurice: I want a divorce.

HUNNI

Hermit Crabs

You are different people, depending on who you are with. You know this and you even know when you are self-censoring; you have that awareness. It's always with family and with work, never when you go for long walks on the beach. They are your three groups and your three personalities: family, the beach and work. You expect it's the same for everyone but maybe worse for you than others because you are prone to living inside your head. It's an occupational hazard, for at least one of your jobs. You work two jobs. The one that pays the soul is the sea shell job. The one that – surprisingly – pays the rent is the retail job.

In retail you are paid to agree with anything the customer says, unless they say that they look bad in a dress, or a pair of pants makes their bum look big. In that case, you are paid to lie.

You are aware that the list of things you are agreeing with is getting longer and more disturbing. Last week, a woman came in to buy a dress and complain about her son's teacher.

Or maybe she came in to complain about her son's teacher, and buy a dress. Either way, she did one and not the other. You found yourself agreeing that teachers are lazy for having days off to write reports. 'Why should they be given a day off to do their jobs? If I asked for a day off to do my job, I'd be laughed at.'

You found yourself nodding at the women who said that chemists should sell bullets over the counter, made available free of charge to all the nut jobs who need anti-psychotic drugs to 'save us all the trouble and expense of futile rehabilitation'.

You found yourself agreeing that climate change was 'hooey' and the government just wanted to screw more money out of us. This lady bought a six-hundred-dollar sequined gown, made in Italy.

You found yourself wishing for that bullet, for yourself, by the end of the day.

It is hard to find complete shells these days. You have to go further and further out, away from metropolitan beaches, and you have to plan for the tides. The waning of a high tide is the only time worth going now. Or after a storm. You find yourself increasingly drawn to other detritus among the shells and wonder if you can make something of it. You talk to your other boss, the man who owns the pet shop in the mall, and he laughs like you are joking until he realises you are not and then he looks at you deliberately for a long moment before turning to a customer.

He says, 'Can I help you with anything?'

You decide to try the idea that is forming in your mind. There are fewer shells, anyway. You know that the pet shop owner can import shells, painted with just as much skill as yours are, but he does not. Yet. Maybe this kind of innovation might save your soul-job. Maybe once he sees that it can be beautiful he will change his mind. You found a curl of broken glass the other day. Its edges were smoothed after years at sea and its frosted green skin glowed when held up to the light. You decide that if it had been the neck of the bottle it would have been perfect. You keep your eyes out.

You decide to experiment with shell designs. Mostly people want beach scenes. They assume hermit crabs want to live in shells that look something like their natural habitats. They're wrong. You have had pet hermit crabs since you were thirteen and know that they have no such scruples. They choose a house because it fits, because it is the right shape for them, right now. Because they can tuck themselves in and out as they please. Not because it is blue like the ocean, yellow like the sand or some combination of the above. You discover, very quickly, that the shells you adorn with diamantes sell like cherries before Christmas. You discover, very quickly, that shells with skulls and crossbones sell – you assume to young boys with pirate obsessions. You discover that floral designs sit, unwanted, for a long time and eventually get handed back for you to 'rework'. You add diamantes to the stamens. They sell very quickly. It's not so hard to change people's views on hermit crab shells, you discover. Now, no one wants ocean pictures. It's like mobile phone covers: a hermit crab shell is an extension of the owner's personality. And you can change it. Every time your crab grows, you can change its shell like you are changing your dress. A crab can go from a semi-stormy beach scene (by far the most popular of all beach scenes) to wearing a schooner of beer or a necklace of pearls. Suddenly the possibilities of self-expression are endless. You like this idea.

You start to paint shells for yourself. You line them up on your dresser like some women line up beauty products. You start with three, for your three personalities. The shell you take to the dress shop is painted black; it's symbolic of the dark void you feel when you are there, the void that makes it easier to lie to your customers. The shell you take to the beach is painted pink, the colour of acceptance and calm. The shell you take when you visit your family is yellow, which you are pleased to learn on The Meaning of Colour dot com means both joy and deception. You wonder if it's strange that you don't paint anything other than a solid colour, then you remind yourself that these shells are just for you, and it is okay.

And then you meet someone who you think you might like and you take him home. Occasionally, you find that you self-censor with him. You don't know where this fits. You do not self-censor all the time, like at work or with family, but there isn't the same ease that you feel on the beach. He fits somewhere in the middle. You go to The Meaning of Colour dot com and consult the charts, trying to find a colour that fits him. There is no single colour. He's a little bit red (because there is passion) and he's a little bit orange (because he has energy that is never quite exhausted). There is brown (because he is stable, earth-like, reliable). You want to add green for harmony and family but you know it is too early. There cannot be harmony when there is self-censoring.

You find yourself self-censoring when he asks about your shells one night.

'What are these?'

'Oh, that's just for work.'

'For the dress shop? Is it some kind of summer promotion? I hope they pay you for your out-of-hours.'

'No, not for the dress shop.'

'What then?'

'I paint them, for hermit crabs. The pet shop sells them.'

He laughs. Like he's never met a person who did such a ludicrous and useless thing.

You blush. It's a different red to the one you normally associate with him. This time it's shame, not passion.

'Oh, Hunni, I'm sorry. It's just...I've never thought about who does that stuff. I assumed it was done overseas, you know, in sweatshops. Not here, not in our sweatshop.'

He leans in, suggestively. You thank God he doesn't wink. You want to tell him to leave, but you let him kiss you.

After that you wonder if his true colour is white: the colour of mourning in eastern cultures. His family came to Australia from Malaysia. With his eyes like rigidly frilled cone fish shells and his laconic Australian drawl, he exists in two worlds. That was why you liked him in the first place. Right now he makes you feel white.

You take your idea to the pet shop owner. Single colour shells. Sold with a colour chart next to the box, so people can select the meaning they want and then the shell they want. Simplicity in this complex, chaotic world.

'I don't think it will sell, but you can give it a go. On consignment.'

You agree.

You still haven't found a nice smooth bottle neck and you

think that maybe that's just a pipe dream. You laugh at your own half-joke. You decide to tell the multi-coloured man. It is a test.

'I want to paint bottle necks, for the crabs. They're beautiful when they are worn down by the sea.'

'Why'd you bother? It's just junk.'

He has failed the test. You persist; you want him to pass. You think of all his colours: red, orange, brown, white and wonder if you could love someone who has those four colours.

'Not to me.'

'Hunni, it's junk, however you look at it. Why don't you focus on the dress shop? I bet you could be manager if you tried.'

'I don't want to be manager.'

'No one gets on in this world by painting shells.'

You don't speak at all. You tuck yourself into your bottle neck.

POPPY

Dear Diary

Dear Diary,
(If you are reading this Jamie, piss off, this is none of your business and if I find out you read this I will tell Tarnya you dream about her every night, moaning her name so loud it wakes up the dog. Go on. Try me. I dare you.)

Today at school Michelle, Naomi, Gemma, Lucy, Kira and me talked about which movies we were going to see in the holidays, and which subjects we would take next year. Gemma is so serious. She's taking maths 1 & 2, physics, chem and for a lark, biology. She wants to be an engineer. Sounds like my idea of hell, but then I guess my subjects probably sound like hell to her.

Okay. That's probably enough to have bored Jamie by now. But IF you are still reading this Jamie, this is your last chance. You bloody better piss off. Or the wrath will come down upon thee.

Dear Diary,

At lunch time today Tarnya came up to us and asked about Jamie. She's a year above us so it's strange that she would speak to us at all — no one ever speaks to anyone below their year level unless it's with some evil purpose. She has this *stride* about her — long, fast steps, like she's in a hurry and she's going to mow down anyone in her path. It screams — *get outta my way, punk!* So naturally, when she walked up to us, we all parted like the Red Sea to make room for her to pass. But she didn't. She stopped just in front of me and started talking.

'Are you Poppy, Jamie's little sister?'

'Yeah.'

'Does he have a girlfriend?'

'How would I know? I'm not his keeper.'

I felt totally badass saying that to Tarnya, but I didn't like the way she just strode up to me and demanded personal information. Who did she think she was?

'Well, do you think you could find out?' she snarled at me.

'Who's asking?' I said.

'That's need to know — and *you* don't need to know.'

'No deal,' I said.

I turned back to the girls and saw their expressions — fear mixed with awe. It made me smile. High school sucks — all these hierarchies and rules about who you are allowed to talk to. I'm over it and I'm not playing anymore.

I heard Tarnya stalk off. Good. She could stew for a while.

Dear Diary,

(Same deal, Jamie. Piss off. Or I will tell Tarnya you have an eye for the boys.)

Today, Tarnya's *friend* came up to us. I don't know her name.

'So what gives? How come you won't tell Tarnya if he has a gf?'

'Why doesn't she ask him herself? He's got ears and a mouth. He can talk for himself.'

'You don't know anything, do you? You're such a baby, Poppy.'

'*I'm* the baby?'

That really made me laugh – *I'm* the baby in this scenario? I might only be fourteen but I am so much older than high school.

The friend strode off, without even half the attitude of Tarnya. Clearly had a long way to go in bitch training.

Dear Diary,

(Piss *off* Jamie, or I will tell Tarnya you have herpes. Which you caught off the dog. I mean it.)

Well today was one for the books. Jamie walked up to Tarnya at lunchtime. Michelle, Naomi, Gemma, Lucy and I were watching from across the courtyard. Jamie walked straight up to her like he had balls of steel, all macho-like and confident. Chest puffed out, hair slicked back, walking like a giant. I couldn't hear what was said, of course, but I can guess. Here's how it would have gone.

'Hi Tarnya, how's it going?'

'Who are you?'

'Jamie. We've got history together.'

Pause.

'I, ah, I mean the class. With Mr Edleston?'

Beat.

'So?'

'So, I was wondering if, you know, you'd like to go see a movie this weekend?'

'With you?'

'Yeah, with me.'

'I've got a boyfriend, doofus. What did you say your name was again? Jamie? I might just tell Nathaniel you're hitting on me.'

(I don't know her boyfriend's name. They say he goes to Saints. I'm sure he'd have to have a tosser name like Nathaniel.)

'Sorry, I didn't know... I'll just leave you alone.'

'Too fucken right you will,' Tarnya said with a flick of her hair (this part I saw, from across the courtyard, so I know she did that).

That's when you turned and walked away, didn't you Jamie?

So from now on, when I say DON'T READ MY DIARY I mean it. PISS OFF!

JENNIFER AND AVA

Patchwork

Ava's nappy is leaking. Wiping green-yellow smears from her thighs, back and stomach, I wonder if it's possible to clench my nose. I shut my eyes against it for a moment and a face appears: tight jaw, shadows like caves above and under his cheek bones, deep set blue eyes hidden by a long blonde fringe. Alexander.

My spirit flickers small, like fireflies in the darkest part of a cave, but I won't go back there.

I finish the job as Ava hums happily at me. She's never struggled on the change table the way some kids do. She watches me and smiles. Her eyes, brown and large like Dan's, seek mine. She is greedy for me.

Stuffing the wipes into the plastic bag, I say, 'There we go!', and plonk her on the floor. Off she trundles towards the kitchen, making straight for the saucepan drawer. She grabs the lids and starts whacking them together. Harmless, I think, and head for the studio sunroom.

The horizon canvas I've been staring at for a week still

eludes me entirely. It's empty, and not in a good way. I can't find the answers because I don't even know the right questions.

From the kitchen, Ava cries. Sharp-edged disasters and panic run like arrows through my mind as I bolt back to her.

She stands in front of the fridge, covered in goo, staring at the floor where a dozen eggs have smashed and spread in a viscous muck-pool. The look in her eyes says, 'I'm sorry, Mumma, I'm sorry,' but she's too distraught to do anything but cry. I want to join her, but that would mean surrendering and I may never make it back from there, so I hold on and reach for the paper towels and begin the mop up.

A distant thought occurs to me: comfort her first. But I can't.

The towels get soaked too fast. I give up and lay them over the mess in a soggy patchwork.

Falling in love with Dan felt like creating a patchwork. He grabbed my attention with his large brown eyes and just the way he looked at me made me trust him. I trusted *this* part of him, then another part, then another part, until I trusted him entirely. Little moments built security. I didn't know it then, but security and love are not the same.

LIA, AMOS AND PETE

How to Flirt

Amos's wife is at the bar. Her short blonde hair with its brown roots, her long tanned limbs and athletic waist are trained on the man in front of her. It's summer and Lia is dressed in her favourite way – exposed skin showing off her hard work at the gym. Everything about Lia's body looks familiar to Amos; it is almost like watching himself.

Lia flirts with the man at the bar. She throws her head back and laughs in her deep, raw way that layers joy with sex. She rests a long-fingered hand on the man's shoulder and lets it linger there while she listens to him speak. She raises her champagne to her lips as he raises his beer to his, and lets her hand slip lower onto his bicep, gripping it a little more tightly now, no longer resting. Lia has perfected an almost clinical flirtation process, but it is her intuition that really makes her good at it.

Amos turns his attention to the man now. His body language is just as important as Lia's. In fact, everything rests on his reaction. The man is leaning against the bar and his hips are pointing in Lia's direction. This is one of the signs Lia has told Amos to look out for; 'If he's pointing his groin towards me, he's interested – don't bother looking at his face. It's different for men and women – for women, look at their face, for men, look at where their dick is pointing.' So this is good, the man is responding to Lia's flirtation. He smiles when she smiles, laughs when she laughs, drinks when she drinks. This is another sign that Lia has taught him to look for; 'If he's copying my actions, he's interested, if he's looking over my shoulder he's wondering if he can get someone better.'

The man is now touching Lia's back. His hand rests gently on the small of her spine, a finger casually inching through the belt loop at the top of her short denim skirt. This is good; 'If his touch goes a little bit further than mine, it's a good sign. If I touch his arm, he touches my back. If I touch his chest, he touches my arse.' Lia's mantras are a checklist in Amos's mind.

Tonight is going to plan, but the next step is crucial. Amos waits.

They finish their drinks and place the empty glasses on the bar. Amos watches the man closely and knows he is asking Lia if she'd like another drink. This is the moment. Amos knows what his wife is about to say, and it has to be just right. Some men bolt at this point, although Lia is usually pretty good at picking.

And there it is – Lia leans in to whisper in his ear so that her words can't be overheard. She puts her hand on his arm to steady him and keep him close. Her perfume is drifting up from between her breasts as she speaks. She is speaking slowly, with confidence and just a touch of vulnerability, although she possesses none of this particular quality herself, just the ability to portray it when required. She is measuring her words, weighing each one. Certain syllables require gentleness, others require force. Others require sexiness – sexiness is Lia's trump card.

There are a couple of ways this could play out. Sometimes, but not often, the man pulls away as though he's been slapped in the face, looks wild enough to punch Lia and then storms away breathing words like 'disgusting', 'pervert' and 'slag'. More often than that, though, and because Lia has a knack for picking them, the man looks over to where Lia is pointing, towards Amos, and checks him out. At this point, Amos's role is simple: raise his glass in their direction, give a small smile and hold the man's gaze. The message is clear, 'I'm in. Are you?' Then it is all up to the man.

As predicted, the man follows Lia's gaze and looks at Amos. He looks for a long time. Amos holds his gaze, just as Lia has taught him to. He is starting to feel anxious.

Amos sees a faint smile appear on the man's face and he feels his excitement build. This one looks just right, for them both. He signals for Amos to come to the bar and join them.

Amos watches as his wife pulls the thin cotton sheet away from the small sweating child asleep in bed. After a night like they've had, he is always astonished that she can switch back to motherhood so easily. Lia turns and leaves the room where their two sons sleep peacefully, and goes to pay the babysitter. It is 3am: an expensive night out, even considering the drinks that the man bought for them.

Amos follows Lia to the kitchen and watches as she makes a cup of tea for each of them.

'It was a good night, don't you think?' she says over the boiling kettle.

'You chose well, you always do.'

Lia smiles, 'I've had some practice now. I know the ones who will get it, and the ones who won't. I can tell just by watching them for a while.'

'But still, it's brave.'

Lia shrugs.

Lia pours the drinks and puts the cups on the table in front of Amos, then sits on his lap, ignoring the way the arms of his chair gouge her legs. Beneath her, Amos knows she can feel his spindly and wasted legs, but he cannot feel her weight at all.

'We can stop this anytime you want, you know,' Lia says.

'You say that every time. But you know I like to imagine it's me you're with,' says Amos.

'Yes, but...'

'I know, I'll tell you if it ever changes for me. And you will tell me too.'

Lia leans over and kisses her husband. 'Of course. Shall we go to bed?'

'Sure,' Amos says.

Lia leaves their drinks on the table and wheels her husband into their bedroom. She helps him into his pyjamas and into bed. Because she knows he's tired, she arranges his legs so that they can spoon and puts her arm around him, resting it in the valley where his ribs give way to his waist. There she can feel his chest rising and falling more and more slowly as he falls asleep in her arms.

Need

The phone rings. I keep breathing.

'Hello?'

'Hey, how're you doing, Lia?'

Keep breathing.

'Sorry. Stupid question.'

'I wonder how many times I've heard the word "sorry" in the last six weeks? You could probably give me a formula for it, couldn't you?' I say.

'Probably.' His laugh has an anxious edge.

Phone calls are awful for this kind of thing: the silences.

'How are the boys holding up?' he asks.

'Oh, they're not. Not really. But they're better than me,' I say.

'Lia, I – .'

'Pete, can you come over? The boys are with their grandma and I just need something more human than the telly tonight.'

I make an effort to clean myself up. Since Amos' funeral I've lived in tracksuits that are faded or stained. I have enough pride to pull myself out of my grief-lethargy, even if it is only for one night.

The knock at the door startles me and the lipstick I am attempting to apply jolts a fat pink line up my cheek. My jeans and jumper are a pitiful attempt to be normal: the smeared lipstick seems to suit my state of mind so much better. For a moment I consider leaving it, answering the door just like that. Pete wouldn't mind. He's seen me worse.

No he hasn't.

Tears run down my face. I dab them with a tissue, using the damp fibres to wipe off the lipstick.

Opening the door, we look at each other and hug awkwardly. Already I know something has changed between us.

In the kitchen, I put on the kettle. Pete opens the fridge and plucks out a bottle of wine. He chooses glasses from the cabinet – two of them – and pours them to the rim. I let the kettle boil.

'How's Sandra?' I ask. 'Did she mind you dropping everything to come rescue me?'

'Sandra doesn't mind what I do these days. Since she moved out I haven't been up the top of her list.'

There is a snag of guilt in my gut: I've been a bad friend.

'Pete, I'm sorry. I didn't know.'

'Hey, it's okay. You've had bigger stuff on your mind.'

We both take a gulp of wine.

'So Riley said to me the other day, "Do I still belong to Daddy, Mum?". And I said, "Yes, of course, darling, you always will". And then he said, "Are you still my grown-up, Mum?"'

Pete reaches out and touches my shoulder. I feel his hand cold from the wineglass, through my jumper.

'I don't feel like the grown-up anymore. I don't want to be.'

'I don't remember ever hurting much as a kid. Apart from when I broke my arm...' Pete says.

We move to the lounge room. We choose opposite couches. People often got the wrong idea about the two of us so it was easier for all concerned – especially our partners – if we just kept our distance. Now our habits are embedded.

I curl my legs up, uncomfortable in my jeans.

'You know this is the first time I've been out of tracky dacks since the funeral,' I say.

'Lia, you don't have to be together, no one expects you to be.'

'Riley and Ethan do.'

'Do you think they care what you wear?'

'It's symbolic, Pete.'

'It's just clothes.'

Somewhere in that exchange is a weak echo of how Pete and I used to be.

'Do you know why I wanted you to come over tonight, Pete?'

'I assume it's because you want to fuck me.'

Our standard joke. People think men and women can't be friends. Pete and I relished ambushing that idea by calling their bluff. Amos and Sandra had been in on the joke.

But tonight it isn't a joke. I need to feel something other

than grief and all I can think about is fucking. There is no one else I trust enough. Pete and I have never so much as kissed before, but tonight I want him. It is selfish and I don't like to admit it to myself, but I've orchestrated this whole thing. The boys sleeping over, the wine in the fridge, the condoms by the bed. Somewhere in my muddled mind I'd planned *this* when I couldn't even plan getting out of my tracksuit. The guilt feels like a hypodermic needle to my heart. I can't feed my boys more than toast and jam. Did I actually leave the house to buy condoms? I should be steaming vegetables and talking about Daddy always being with us in our memories.

The tears ransack my whole body. Pete comes to me and holds me tight. He is rocking me gently and whispering, 'I'm sorry, it was our joke, I'm sorry.'

I stop crying. His arms are strong, his back thick with muscle. I've never noticed his smell before. It is a combination of faded aftershave and something garlicky.

Maybe this is enough, I think. I will just hold him. I haven't been held by a man for so long and it feels so good it almost hurts. The tide is ebbing away, for now at least.

He stops whispering and starts stroking my hair. It was something my mother used to do when I was a kid, and Pete knows it soothes me. He's never done it to me before, but we've talked about it. We've talked about everything.

I don't want to be soothed. I take his hand and stop him, pull back just far enough to see his face. His brown eyes are bloodshot and that only makes me want him more.

I kiss him, tentatively because I don't know how to kiss another man and I don't want to kiss Pete the way I had kissed Amos. With Amos it had become perfunctory towards the end, when it was hard for him even to offer me his lips.

Pete doesn't respond. I can feel him subtly pulling away, not wanting to kiss me but too fearful to stop my madness. There are no words for it so I keep kissing him, drawing him, thread by thread, into my need.

And then kissing him stops working. I need to be lost, engulfed, subsumed. He lets me take off his shirt. His chest is smooth and then that delicate skin on my hands isn't enough. I take off his pants and feel the coarse hair on his legs. It gives me a moment of satisfaction, but then it is gone. I feel like an addict, clawing for more even as I get more. He doesn't stop me, but he doesn't *do* anything either. Is he going to perform a sacrificial function? Do me a favour? This isn't right, I need a connection. I stop kissing him and force him to look at me. He's crying.

He finally touches me and too soon it is done and we lay down, face to face, breathing each other's air as we sleep.

When I wake, crumpled and cramped on the narrow ledge of the couch, I am alone. Pete has returned to the other couch, curled into a tight ball, and turned away from me.

JENNIFER AND DAN

Cat food and snappyhappy stories

One of my old commercials comes on the telly. Cat food. Vivaldi's 'Winter' plays as the fur-ball (white as snow) ambles aimlessly around the (white as snow) backdrop, apparently unimpressed with life, until she spots the bowl of food. She speeds up, still managing to look languid and aloof. Takes a haughty sniff. Tucks in. Cue logo.

We had to drizzle honey over the food to make her eat it.

Dan looks over at me and smiles. He remembers the story about the honey.

'Didn't that cat scratch the entire crew raw that day?' he asks.

'Yep. She looks divine but she's pure evil.'

He reaches for the remote.

'Do you mind?'

I shake my head, no, and he flicks, murmuring to himself, 'Fifty-seven channels and nothing on.'

He pauses on SBS, looking for a doco, but there's nothing there either.

'Any word on them finally screening "Kids Behind Bars"?' he asks.

'No. Apparently we're saturated with detention stories. Compassion fatigue, they call it. They want something different. Something happy. "Snappy and happy" is actually what the commissioning editor said to me.'

'But they bought it. Why don't they just put it on?'

'Your guess is as good as mine,' I say.

I can't be bothered trying to explain to Dan how the system works. It's nice of him to show an interest in my work, but he's never done it before, beyond the necessities of my travel itineraries. Now he's clutching at relationship straws and it smells of desperation. We're looking for dusty conversation at the bottom of a drought-stricken lake.

'Do you think you might make one of those snappyhappy docos? Or maybe some more ads?'

'Ava's only 18 months,' I say. 'Are you worried about money?'

'No, not so much…'

There's something else he wants to say, so I wait.

'I know that you're busy, don't get me wrong, I know Ava's a full time job and then some. It's just that I wonder if you're…bored?'

Bored. The word stops me. Do I have the right to be bored? Isn't what I'm doing too important to be boring? It's too hard to think about, so I change the subject.

'I don't think I can make those sorts of films again. It seems unbearable now, to immerse myself in human misery. I don't have the fight in me anymore.'

'What about the snappyhappy stories, then?'

'Is there such a thing?'

I look over at Dan, in his pyjamas already, even though it's only 8pm. I try to conjure some feeling towards him, something *warm*, but there is nothing. No hatred, but no love either. Is there such a thing as a complete absence of feeling in a marriage? It's not supposed to work that way. Shouldn't I at least be mad at him?

There's nothing snappyhappy about the look Dan is giving me, nor about the look I'm giving him, I suppose. I've slipped into the cracks of my life and it's dark in here. Dan turns to the remote and settles on a channel – reality TV somethingorother.

DONNA AND DAMIEN

Jesus and the Tsunami

Donna and Damien sit on a rolled-up swag in the tray of Damien's ute, huddled against the bellowing, cantankerous wind. Behind them is the headland: a colossal cyst on the arid landscape of the peninsula just out of town. Gulls swoop and dive in the winds that squall up the cliff. In the water the last surfer of the day dangles his legs over the sides of his board.

The swig Donna takes from the can of bourbon premix fizzes down her throat. She passes the can to Damien and watches his long hair get all caught up in the wind, his fringe upright in shards like the jagged volcanic rocks below them, before abruptly falling flat over his face. He's wearing his 'fuck you world' expression.

'I feel like I could jump off the cliff and fly. Lift off with the wind,' says Donna.

Damien ignores her.

'How'd you go today, Don?' He is asking about her job, but Donna doesn't want to think about that now.

'S'alright,' she shrugs. 'Nothing to say, hey.'

He turns away and his fringe whips up and flies into the air. *Take off!* Donna wishes she could do that. *Take off!*

She knows Damien is waiting for her to ask about his old man. She doesn't want to think about that either.

'Whadya reckon would happen if one of them waves came here, you know, like in Japan or New York? One a them huge motherfuckers that wipes out the whole city? Even the Drive would be gone, wiped off the face of the planet,' Donna says.

'Them waves won't ever come here, nothing to wipe out. Be pointless.'

Donna laughs and the sound of it is carried away, over the ochre cliff and into the quiet cove behind them where old fishers pull in nets dangling with crabs.

'Nah, seriously, if it did. And we were up here. We might be the only people left. If one of them waves came right now, *boom!* and wiped out everything in the whole sorry place. Then the tide got sucked back out to sea, and took them all with it. People, houses, dogs and cats. Then what?'

'Christ, Don, you're bloody tragic tonight.'

'I know.'

She takes a drag. Her cigarette is almost gone, even though she's only just lit it.

'Bloody wind,' she says.

The lone surfer paddles to shore.

'Shark bait's comin' in,' says Damien.

'He'd be dead,' Donna says with a nod of her head.

'Ease up, babe,' Damien says. 'D'ya wanna go get a pizza?'

'No money.'

'My shout,' Damien says.

'Alright then. A bit later, hey.'

Donna thinks about all the old people down there at sea level and doesn't want to go back down just yet.

'Me old man's back in hospital,' Damien says.

'I'm sorry, babe,' she says, but secretly she wishes he hadn't told her. She'd been imagining a wave the size of a ten-storey building crashing down on her parents' house, smashing it into toothpicks. She pictures her collie, Jesus, old now and imagines him clinging to a piece of smashed plasterboard and making it to dry land while her parents and big brother drown in a turban-swirl of foaming, angry water.

'What's it this time?'

'Tumour's back. They said he wouldn't survive another one.'

Damien's eyes are glistening. It might be the wind. Donna wonders if he'd want his family saved from the wave or if he'd be happy if they drowned. His dad's a prick, but he's dying now and that changes everything.

Donna takes the can from Damien's hand. She stamps her cigarette butt out on the floor of the ute tray and takes a swig.

'Who would you bring up here if you knew a wave was coming? Who'd you want to be stuck with in this washed-out shithole for the rest of your life?'

'Hell, Don.'

'I'm just sayin'...'

'Well, don't. Just bloody don't.'

'You worried about your dad?' Donna sighs.

'Nah, mate. It's all over for him. He's cactus. It's Mum I'm worried about.'

'What'll she do?'

Donna thinks that if she was Damien's mum she'd

probably chuck a party when the old fella kicked it, but she figures Damien doesn't want to hear that right now.

'I'd bring you up here. You and Jesus,' he says.

Donna smiles. She knows he only said it to make her feel better. But even that's something.

JIMMY AND ANDY

The Bedside Cinema

The Bedside Cinema, opposite the old theatre they are pulling down, used to be a church but the priests abandoned the building and in came the porn stars. They kept the pews and the pulpit, for those patrons with God issues, and added a silver screen.

Sitting in the back row, underneath the projectionist's booth, I can see the smoke stains from the votive candles.

I catch an unexpected smell and look around to see where it's coming from. It smells like fire. The whole audience – there are seven of us day-time viewers – notice. It takes everyone's eyes from the screen at a critical moment in the 'plot', if you know what I mean. A man in the front row stands, puts his hands on his hips – his silhouette shows a bulge in his pants – and swings his torso from side to side as he looks for the source of the smell. Others follow suit – showing off their erections, putting their hands on their hips and swaying their torsos. Like some sort of horny aerobics warm up. One of them looks like Andy, but I can't be sure.

I don't have an erection to show off. (In fact, I have been questioning why I still come to this place. It never seems to do anything for me anymore.) I stay in my seat, which makes me look guilty. Everyone stops swaying and points their erections at me. It is very threatening.

Their stares incriminate me and I want to say something. ('It's okay, I didn't summon the fire. It wasn't me!') ('Do you think we are damned?') But I keep my mouth shut and spin my head from side to side, looking from the vestibule to the pulpit, seeking answers. The men, hands still on hips, turn to look at each other in a coordinated movement that is so silken that it might just be preordained.

Light flickers behind them as the movie splutters and splurges through the first orgasm scene, and white overtakes flesh as whole frames disappear into blinding silvery nothingness. The amplified moans and groans stop and start as the movie flickers in and out until the woman and her fireman have disappeared into a hot glow, illuminating every dust mote on every pew and every frayed edge of velvet curtain and every candle smoke stain on the wall. The light fills the room with heat too, and, as panic starts to rise, I understand the strange smell – the film has burned up, it has been razed as it whirled through the spool, too hot for its own good.

Intense light spills from the projection room. I stand (my fear of being burned alive has finally overtaken my embarrassment at not being aroused) and run out from under the projection room to get a better look at what is going on. The others, who are no longer pointing with their genitals, follow my gaze. Our heads lift to the high raked ceilings, into the room where the images are projected onto the screen, from which a pure light is emanating gloriously. It is not fire, it is too bright. I squint and shield my eyes from the searing light. The others are all in prayer, heads bowed against the glare. Or perhaps they are cowering in fear.

Then the light splits, a peach's flesh under a knife, and a figure appears in the booth. A woman.

'It's the woman from the film!' someone calls.

'You're an idiot!' I say to the man. 'Are you okay up there?' I call up to the projection room.

She waves, or at least I think she's waving. Then a burst of white smoke comes from her hands and I realise she's waving a fire extinguisher over the flames of the celluloid.

'Can I help you? How can I get up there?' I yell at her, but she ignores me. I wouldn't want me up there either, if I was her. It's obvious I'm a creep. But I'm also a sort of professional broadcaster, so we are sort of contemporaries and I feel responsible.

I race to the back of the theatre, push open the door that says 'No Entry Staff Only,' and follow the flight of stairs up to the projection booth. The smoke gets thicker with each step, the smell of burning film acrid and abrasive. Opening the door to the booth, smoke billows out like a parachute filling with air, covering me, suffocating.

'Are you okay?' I yell again.

'Over here!' she shouts back. I fight my way through the smoke to get to the other side of the booth.

She passes me an extinguisher and I fumble with it, inept and useless, as usual, at important tasks. I hear Andy telling me I'm shit, I'm pointless, I'm a dick. But I push him down, hard. Finally I figure out the pin, and depress the handle and the white powder billows out. It throws me against the wall. But the fire is dying out and the woman grabs me by the arm.

'C'mon let's get out of here. There's too much smoke.'

Following her down the stairs, I'm convinced she is some kind of superhero. Back on the ground floor, the sirens wail in the near distance.

'Kind of ironic, don't you think?' I say to the woman. 'A film about firefighters, and here we are...'

She grimaces at me and turns to walk towards the fire fighter.

Her disdain is obvious and it stings. But what do I expect? She's a superhero and I'm a creep and a weirdo and just smart enough to know it, which makes me the worst kind of creepy weirdo.

I hang around to answer the firefighter's questions, and then the police's questions and overhear conversations about the place being beyond repair, likely to be demolished. Looking along Plane Tree Drive, the trees are in full orange glory and I'm glad the fire didn't spread. Those leaves would have been perfect tinder and is such a nice place to live, aside from the smouldering old church cum porno theatre on the corner.

Community Radio

'Hey Jude' is playing. I fought with Andy over whose 'Hey Jude' we should play. He wanted his CD version, but of course that's only because he doesn't remember how to queue up vinyl. But what's 'Hey Jude' with the chemical gloss of a CD?

The track ends and I hit Mic 1 and Mic 2.

"Hey Jude', for all you Beatles fans. And you know, Andy, wasn't that better than that CD version? C'mon Andy, be honest with Jimmy.'

'Jimmy, only tossers refer to themselves in the third person. Queue the next track. This is Nine Inch Nails with a number that *was* recorded for CD. Press the damn button, Jimmy.'

Andy gets up from his chair, throws his headphones onto the desk with more than his usual disdain, and flops onto the green vinyl couch in the corner of the studio. He shuts his eyes and his arm dangles over the edge of the couch onto the floor like a lazy ape. I don't know how he can even sit on that couch; it must have been from the 1950s and had never once been cleaned. The foam stuffing is bursting out of it like pus from a green blister and whenever anyone sits on it puffs of dust form clouds like a swarm of micro-beasts. It is rank.

'You're on 89.9 Community Radio, it's three-thirteen am on the knocker, here're the Nails,' I say as I watch Andy become engulfed in the ancient spores of the couch.

'No one's listening, Jimmy, you don't have to sound like such a wad. And no one says 'the Nails'.'

'No one's listening? No one? I beg to differ, my friend. Last week we put a call out and the phones lit up. Two callers.'

'Yeah, I've never been so flat chat in all my life. That was crazy, man.' Andy's eyes flick up to the On Air sign above the studio door, directly in his line of sight from his reclining position on the couch. 'You didn't turn the mics off, for fuck's sake!'

I follow his glance. Andy is right, I haven't turned the mics off. I press the buttons.

'Jesus.'

'Don't worry, like I said, no one's listening.'

'Really?' I ask, pointing to Line 1, flashing red.

'Hello, 89.9 Community Radio,' I say.

'I'm listening.'

The line goes dead.

'What was that?'

'Someone said, "I'm listening" and hung up.'

'Proves my point, only weirdos and freaks listen to community radio at 3am on Thursday morning.'

It is hard to build an argument against Andy on this one. We've been doing this show together for two years now and we've only had a few calls in all that time. The first one was my mum, on my first show. But even she stopped listening after a week or two. After that it was just the odd pot smoker up late requesting 'Dark Side of the Moon'. I'd tested Andy's theory, that no one ever listened, a couple of times by asking a trivia question and offering an old cassingle as a prize. Someone always called up and answered the question and then got shirty 'cause I wouldn't post the cassingle to them – they had to come to the station and pick it up. Don't they know I don't get paid to do this job, unless you count unemployment benefits?

'Someone could break in here and hack us to bits with a cleaver and we could be yelling out a detailed commentary as it happened until the air goes dead when they smash the blood-soaked panel to smithereens and no one would come and save us because *no one is listening*.' Andy says from the couch.

Sometimes I hate Andy. For one thing he always programs these long Nine Inch Nails songs that make my ears want to puke, and for another he has a knack for giving voice to these things that happen to me in my sleep at night. In truth, the only reason I keep him on the show is because I feel a bit safer with someone else around.

'Or, one night, if you don't shut up about 'Hey Jude' maybe *I* might be the one to come in here with a cleaver.'

Andy thinks he is hilarious.

But, seriously, can he read my mind? I'm trying not to feel paranoid, but it is getting harder.

The phone rings again and Andy springs up from the couch, sending up another storm of spores, and grabs it before I can get to it.

'Hello, 89.9 Community Radio, *I'm listening.*' Andy says the last bit in a spooky voice, the kind of voice you use in grade five to scare the girls during a séance.

'Shut up, Andy,' I say, snatching the phone from him. I queue up the next track – 'Ingrid Bergman' by Billy Bragg – and speak to the caller.

'Hello, caller?'

'He's right you know, I could hack you up and no one would know. Not even your mother listens to this show.'

I check the panel – mics are off. This guy, whoever he was, couldn't possibly have heard us. We are in a sound-proof studio for fucks' sake. And anyway, that thing about my mother...I'd only been *thinking* that, hadn't I?

'Who are you?'

I flick my eyes up to Andy, now resting his head on the panel looking lazier than ever – maybe he'd set up one of his loser mates to spook me. I kick him under the desk and he looks up at me. His face shows nothing; no glimmer of a smirk, but no fear either. In fact he looks strangely wax-like.

As Billy spins around, I wait for the caller to answer me.

He hangs up.

'Alright, so who've you set up to call?'

'What're you talking about? I didn't do that.'

As much as I don't want to, I believe Andy. I know his faces – all three of them – and the one he has on now is his 'I don't really give a fuck' face (incidentally, his most common face). That face doesn't lie, because Andy genuinely doesn't give a fuck about most things. He's gone back to playing with his phone – another thing that pisses me off about him. We're supposed to be working.

Billy Bragg is winding up (he's always short and sweet) so I queue up the next track: Martha Wainwright. I just shove it in and hit play. It is unlike me to not carefully select a track and announce it. It's fair to say I'm freaked out.

I look down at the panel to check the sound levels – sometimes Martha needs to be turned up – and see a liquid pooling at the edge of the desk. It is tan, syrupy and, yes, it smells. Bad. Like days old veggie scraps. The liquid spreads, oozing down into the cracks of the panel. I look up at Andy, and he is still fiddling with his phone, oblivious and waxy.

'Andy?' I say, as Martha croons around us.

Andy looks up at me and then pointedly fixes his eyes on his elbows and I can see that *he* is in fact the tan-coloured sludge. It is dripping off him and pooling around his elbows where he's leaned them on the desk. It is running from his elbows and into the panel.

Andy's wax-face has changed. This is not an Andy face I know. It is melting, softly drooping downwards towards his neck. To my horror, his neck is pooling around his chest. His chest is starting to look concave as things slip further and further south.

Grabbing my old windcheater, I use it to mop up the mess, soaking Andy into the fibres as Martha becomes prickly and fuzzy. The panel is dying, I can't mop him up fast enough.

'Andy, help me! At least get your elbows off the desk! Can't you see what's happening?'

I drop the windcheater – it's soaked and useless anyway – and it falls, laden with Andy, to the floor. Andy begins to seep into the coarse fibres of the studio carpet and become indistinguishable from the rest of the dirt that has been trodden into it for decades before us. I panic. I don't want Andy to vanish into the floor – how would I ever get him back again? I rip some old laminated posters from the walls – Beck from his *Loser* days and Regurgitator in their *Unit* era – and put them underneath the windcheater so that Andy can coagulate on the laminate.

It works. I begin to see parts of him forming over the poster images. *Unit* was a good choice – the yellow album cover is a clear backdrop and I see parts of Andy against it.

Martha has stopped and there is dead air all around. It has probably been like that for ages. I do the only thing I can: take a mic, turn it on and start a commentary.

'Ah, sorry for the dead air folks, but the strangest thing just happened. My colleague Andy just melted into the panel. I mopped him up with my windcheater, and when he was all gone, I threw my windcheater onto the floor. He started to... hell! He's coming back! It's okay, folks! I can see him taking shape again. It's starting at the floor, with his shoes. It's slow, but it's happening! He's going to be okay! Andy! Can you hear me mate?'

The phone panel lights up. I pick up Line 1.

'Jimmy, your mum called me. We're putting the plan into action. What's going on there?'

It is Michelle, the station manager.

'Michelle!'

How much did she hear? Was she listening? It was a train wreck, even for the graveyard shift, one hellava train wreck.

'Jimmy...' her voice holds a warning. 'You're still on air. Queue up a track and turn off the mics.'

I do as she says, then go back to the phone.

'All set, Michelle. It's the strangest thing, first there was this call from a guy, he seemed to be reading my mind, and then Andy – '

'Jimmy. I'm sending around some people. They are going to help you. Just stay where you are, okay. Promise me you will stay where you are?'

'Sure, there's still twenty minutes of the show left, I'm not deserting my post! But wait 'til you hear about Andy – '

'Jimmy, Andy hasn't been around for over three years.' Michelle's voice is very calm and soothing. Maybe she just woke up. 'Since before you joined the station. Remember you told me in your interview that if Andy came back I was to call the police? That Andy messed with your head, that you hadn't heard from him for a long time, but that he might come back someday? And that if he did...?'

'If he did?'

I don't want to think about what Michelle is saying. But Andy is back, she's right.

'The ambulance will be there any minute, Jimmy, just hold tight. While we wait, why don't you queue up the emergency tape? I'll walk you through it if you like. We wouldn't want dead air, would we?'

Michelle is right, of course. But I don't need to be told what to do. I know the procedure. I quickly set up the tape.

'Good job, Jimmy. Now, can you leave the studio and walk to the front doors. But stay inside until the ambulance comes.'

'What about Andy? I can't just leave him alone on the floor. Maybe they can help him? The ambulance people?'

'Andy will be just fine, you said he was coming back, didn't you? He will be just fine.'

'I think it was the spores from the couch, you should get that replaced.'

'Yes, you're right, it's a terrible couch. Now, put the phone down and walk to the front, but stay inside until the ambulance comes, okay?'

I do as Michelle instructs. She is very calm and her voice is soothing, and as soon as I leave the sound-proofed studio I can hear the sirens.

I lie on the gurney in the ambulance as they ask me questions.

'Name please?' the paramedic asks.

'Jimmy Absolom.'

'Address?'

'Unit 8, number 1, Plane Tree Drive.'

'Suburb?'

They continue to ask questions and I continue to answer, but as I am talking what I am really thinking about is what Michelle had said about Andy. He *did* always manage to pull himself back together. If it takes him a while to soak out of the carpet and onto the Regurgitator poster and reform into his Nine Inch Nails loving self, well, that isn't such a bad thing. We can do with some time apart.

TIM, ALICE, SUNDANCE AND ARIA

The Rider

The rider is no fun these days: peppermint tea and Cheezels. Nothing worth drinking, snorting, injecting, smoking, sticking up your arse. You love the lows as much as the highs, maybe more. Transcendental nothingness, then a conscious desire to stop breathing. Chasing the dragon even *looked* beautiful – the fiend's dirty tail smoking up into a delicate twist as the gaudy, flamboyant flame licked the foil. There was glory in that.

It's not good to think about this stuff, but sniffing the peppermint tea makes you ache for a hit of damn near anything and your head is in that glamourised lie. You can hear them out there, getting fired up for the gig. The band is hanging out in the corridor, because everyone knows not to bring that stuff into the green room. They are your personal addiction support group – the band, the roadies, the pub management. You're known all across this wide brown land. One slip and you're snowboarding to oblivion. Or drowning in stormwater run-off. You're a precarious soul. They stroke your artistic temperament with a peacock's feather. It keeps them employed. They dance around you like you're gonna break. Because they know you will. Sooner or later.

Out front, the crowd is yelling over Eliza, the support act. Poor girl. A folk singer, pretty and small, faded blonde hair to her waist with just a guitar between her and the hundreds of drunk bastards who have come to hear you scream your anguish into a mic. She needs toughening up. You've had fifteen years of getting bottles hurled at your head in grungy pubs, all the punters judging you on whether you've given them a pound of flesh or a pile of shit. They want flesh, every time. And blood, they want to see you sweat it out of your eyeballs. They want to puke in the carpark afterwards and tell their mates they've never seen anyone be such a God awful fuck-up, but hell the songs kick arse.

That's you – a God awful fuck-up with kick arse songs. Just ask your wife and kids. No need for a crystal ball.

There you go again. Your brain connects dots you're trying to rub out. Now you're thinking about meth.

The tea tastes like flavoured dirt, you'll never get used to it. People who like it are lying to themselves. You spent years drinking cheap flyblown homebrew, Christ, you'd lick the dregs off the floor. But peppermint tea. Hell.

These days you like to start the gig with some spoken word. Sounds cracked, but you're trying to get them to see things are different now. If you're truthful, you're begging them to see you anew, and still like you. You make the poem funny, of course, throw in some local references so they feel loved, and recite it over a lazy drawl from the band so that they think it's a song, not a *fucken poem*. You tell them that tonight's gonna be different. By then they're restless. Shuffling, skolling, sniggering. They're wondering whether they can get a refund. False advertising; Sweeny ain't what he used to be.

Tonight's poem isn't going too well. It's hard to rhyme anything with 'Adelaide'.

City of churches, city of beaches
Wine barrels for Bordeaux, bodies
And sulphuric witches
But Ad-el-aide you give me the shits
I love you and hate you equally to bits
You are trash, you are treasure
But where're you hiding all my pleasure?

It's rotten and you know it. And if you crap on this town they're gonna want to kill you — even though it's technically your town too. And despite it all, you still want to wake up the next day. Something primal in you needs to see what's on the other side. You punish yourself so you have half a chance of waking up cured.

Then, one especially big night, to breathe or not to breathe was no longer your choice and it stopped being fun. It hadn't been fun for years, but you're a slow thinker and it took a while. You'd wake up and there was more that was lost than was there. People stopped pardoning you. You were no longer the happy rogue drunk, the artist whose indiscretions would be expunged with a chart-topper; who could laugh off incidents that mere mortals would be ashamed of. Of course your wife had stopped forgiving you long before everyone else. And to your kids you were just the drunk who slept it off in the back room in between tours.

Now you're awake and the days are long. The nights never end. The breaths keep coming and sometimes you wish they didn't. Days, nights, breathing is colour free, additive free, preservative free. No MSG. There's no sharpness to anything – no sunlight after a bender. Now it's just life in a blender: grey slop and a dull whine.

Wine.

You hear schooners clinking through the door. For all their support, they don't know what that sound does to you. You start to shake.

You pick up the pen and force your grip. Adelaide is not going to get the better of you. There are so many bad jokes, some of them must rhyme. But tonight you can't make them funny, they only sound mean. They already hate you and they don't even know it yet.

There's a knock on the door.

'Timmy, the natives are restless, Eliza is dying out there.'

'Yeah, mate. Hang on.'

You know you could write this fucker if you had a drink in your hand. You know you could rock the gig if you'd had a hit. But tonight you're gonna suck and they're gonna know it. They're gonna go home saying Tim Sweeny's a has-been. They won't even want you on *Rise and Shine.* You'll get a job producing artists who are on the way up, or down, but never at the top. They'll slap you on the back and say 'I grew up listening to you, you were great,' without thinking about what that actually means. And they'll be snorting and smoking and injecting and doing stuff that hasn't even been thought of yet and you'll be gritting your teeth. For the rest of your life, gritting your Goddamn teeth, wishing on a beautiful dragon.

75

Suite 5, Bundaberg City Motel

In the letter you tried to tell her. There were no excuses for why you couldn't do it for her or the kids. Just explanations. They say the truth sets you free, but that's bullshit, the truth's a prison. You've told her the truth and you know it will lock her away.

The funny thing, the thing you never expected, is that everything is dull except for Alice. It's the one thing that seeps through, a kind of punishment, a repentance for all of it. Nearly twenty years of it. You should be buried under the weight of it and sometimes you think you are but you still breathe when you wake up in the morning, rolling over and looking at the bedside table, looking for the taste, knowing it's not there, then there's the fits and sparks of energy through the mental aerobics of needing it, knowing it's not there and finally convincing yourself you can actually keep going without it.

And that's when Alice seeps in. Alice being locked away forever is even worse than knowing there's no taste waiting for you. You can smell her, somewhere in the membranes of your respiratory system is a piece of her, stuck there, a piece of her forever in you. You curl up and make yourself smaller than you already are and focus on feeling Alice in your nose, imagining it's all of her, buried in you waiting for you to say the magic words like she's a genie in a bottle, ready to materialise next to you. You cradle her there, her memory, her smell and you catalogue all the things you did together. You start from the first time you saw her, jumping around at a gig, covered in sweat, hair matted and making her head look too big for her body. You offered to take her backstage to meet the band. She said no, but she talked to you instead and that moment, when she said no, you fell in love. Then you remember the first time you touched, the first time you kissed, the first time you made love. Each of those memories is a layer of skin, protecting you from the world. You remember moving in with her, taking your pathetic possessions to her place and feeling like you didn't have enough stuff to make an impression on her life. It never really looked like you lived there, and you never really did. There was always a gig, there was always a late night and a couch to sleep on. Then the babies. Those moments of finding out together: this week the fingernails grew, this week the eyes opened, and your favourite: this week your baby can hear you. From that week on you sang to them both, it was all you had to give them. Their births were horror stories. Blood, screaming, panic, pain - torture of an ancient, ancient kind. Something in you broke with both of them; you got a little bit more lost. You floated, you flew, you did everything you could to keep your feet off the ground that she walked on. You had nothing of substance to give those kids, apart from wretchedness. Alice became their everything.

You curl up and remember all this, and all the while you smell Alice and you want her back, but then you get up and reread the letter. You've told her you're straight, have been for six months. You put a cheque in the envelope, a meagre amount, but something. You breathe slowly into the envelope, seal it and post it. You imagine it travelling to Alice. Her surprise when she sees the cheque causes her to inhale sharply. She breathes in a part of you. You enter her mouth and are a part of her.

Reruns

Like reruns of a bad show on telly, his habits came and went. I counted them like the hours on a clock. One would pass — though it took longer than an hour or even a day — and then come back again. I knew the people he was with when he was on a habit, and that he would return to me when he was off. Those teeth rotters are fair-weather friends, there for him when he's got a taste to share and off looking for someone else when he doesn't. They came to the house and sometimes smiled apologetically when they saw the children, fatherless and floating. But they still asked, they always asked for him.

He writes when he's on a habit and tries when he's not. When he comes home to me, to the kids, trying to get straight, he doesn't remember who to be, or how to be. How to even hold them. Maybe he thinks they will break, but he looks more breakable than them. Skinny as tin foil, grotty as an unwashed dog. They hug him like he's fragile or maybe like he's smelly, because he is, and he hugs them like they are fragile, because he is. I ache when I see it; every cell in his body is a pin and the kids are the pin cushion, only they push the pins deeper into him. Between it all, no one gets a decent hug.

There's damage that can't be undone. I count it up like the seconds on the clock. They tick past too fast, and just when I get back to 12 and think that maybe he can change — 'cause there's nothing he hasn't done yet and he must be running out of time to live like this — the damn red hand keeps going around, around, around.

Now I'm a catastrophe of responsibilities and exhaustion. Trying not to snap at them when they pine for him, the man who would turn up to sleep it off and then play with them for half an hour before it got too much to be strung out with noisy kids.

It's impossible to hate him, in amongst it all. He's a good man. I still love him. He told me he's gone straight and he's touring. He sends cheques from time to time. He used to pride himself on being bad at managing his finances, like it was a badge. Used to say that it made him a better artist to be shit at everything else. Like being my husband, their father, for example.

I look at other men. None of them measure up to his five feet ten of skin and bones. His oily hair and no-longer cool retro clothes. His pointy shoes — always shiny. And yellow, bloodshot eyes. No one else has that thing he has, that ability to see through life like he's x-raying it. It's his superpower. But it burns a hole in him. No one can live that way and not get scathed by it. The thinness of him; he's been shaved away.

Jacob is just like his dad. Annabelle is like me. She'll

be fine. Unless she marries someone like her dad, God help her. But Jacob. I'd been too busy telling his dad to fuck off and not come back that I didn't see that Jacob was a living breathing replica. From his skinny limbs to his highs and lows. Jacob probably knew he and his dad were peas in a pod and I was pushing one of the peas out.

Last week there was a letter with the cheque. The bastard didn't have the guts to talk to me. I read the letter then food-processed it with a dash of oil, wishing it was him. There are gaps, white lies, but I can fill them in without too much trouble. We remind him of his other life. Going straight was a roller coaster that always ended up where it started. I want to shred what's left of his skinny carcass, but there is an echo in my head: he's gone straight, he's gone straight... He would never have bothered to write to me while he was high. Then, nothing really mattered.

Someone else will get the straight Tim Sweeny. I got the crap one, the one who was always high or always low, never just right.

Into the Rain

He swirled his lemonade inside the sweaty glass. Bubbles spilled over, dribbling down and wetting his fingers. Aria took them off the glass and licked them clean. Withdrawing his hand, he tipped the rest of the drink into his mouth, swilling it around. He stood and walked away.

'It's done, you know,' she called, her voice spiking with hurt.

He flicked his collar up against the cold. Rain spat on his glasses. He took them off and put them in his pocket, tucked his chin into his chest for a while, then decided it was pointless. He pushed his collar down, unbuttoned his shirt. Let it in, what the hell, he thought.

A busker sheltered in an abandoned doorway, plucking his recycled guitar, his toes resting on the peak of the baseball hat he used for donations.

The song stopped Tim in his tracks. He found a note in his pocket and placed it in the hat, under a coin so it wouldn't blow away.

When the song was finished, he spoke.

'You like that song?'

'Nah, it's just easy to play,' the busker said.

Tim was tempted to take the note back, but he just walked away.

The new songs were too miserable to be sung by buskers in doorways and laneways he thought; only sad folks alone in their bedrooms would attempt them. People searching for meaning amongst the overwhelming proof that there was none.

Street lights lit his way through the grubby urban tangle. He took a shortcut through the park, past the rotunda where people got married in sunshine and rain, and walked into the darkness and the bats. He found a spot under a tree, dryish, and sat.

Alice once told him he dreamed things into life, and she was right. Now it was real and had to face up to the world. How does something created from darkness live in light?

He picked up a fallen leaf and crushed it. The damp brown *papier mâché* stuck to his hand.

A little way away a bottle fell onto a path and smashed. A shuffle and giggle, then bodies crashed to the dirt.

He got up, walked to the tram. At the beach, he listened to familiar inky waves he couldn't see. Leaning against the guard rail, he pushed into the wind.

Gulls flew against the weather in suspended animation.

'Thought you'd be here. I s'pose this is your spot. Your Inspiration Point.'

He turned. Aria, her white skin almost aglow in the vague moonlight.

'Something like that. I wrote the album here. Well, in my head I was here. Even when I was in a hotel room or a bus or at home on the Drive, or...'

'You can say it. With Alice.'

'Yeah.'

'Is this where it happened?'

'Nah.'

'I was sure it was here..."you stood at the edge of the land/ you wouldn't take my hand".'

'That's just a lyric.'

'Oh. Hey, the rain's stopped. I'm freezing, let's go home. We can steal figs and peel them like grapes. C'mon, it'll be fun!'

She held her arm out to him, wiped a spot of rain from her cheek and shivered before folding her arms around her waist.

'C'mon, we'll stoke the radiator, make some coffee and put on Otis Redding,' she said.

Aria didn't seem to care that he was broken. She still saw something left in him that could be coddled back. Perhaps she was right. Maybe another place and another person might feel like home again. Somewhere far away from Alice. His children. Reminders.

He stepped towards her and wrapped her up in his wet jacket.

'Figs? Where're we gonna find figs?' he said.

Fast Forward

Nearly forty. Husband Missing In Action. Body no longer firm. If only I'd known then what I know now. Now my traitorous skin gives me plenty to care about but I just don't. I don't care.

Break away. Rerun. Reinvent.

The kids are staying at Mum's, although Annabelle is disgusted at the idea – she's twelve and thinks she's old enough to be on her own. She probably is, there was never an older twelve-year-old than Annabelle, with all that she's seen. The older she gets, the more capable, the more I want to wrap her up. I never did it when she was a kid; I was brave then. Now I feel her slipping away and I want to pull her in.

Turning the Top 40 music up loud, I dress and dance around my room like a teenager. It's a kick in the teeth to Tim. He hated that music, or anything that was designed to make you feel good, or at least not to think. Freedom wells, making my toes tingle. My house is a blur as I spin – the green silk cushions my grandma made when she was a young wife, the lacy sheers that I've always hated, the floral carpet that is so pounded down by feet that it's almost as hard as floorboards. The vinyl couch Tim brought to our first shared house, the only piece of furniture he ever owned. We used to slip off it in the summer, our sweat pooling in the creases. Now one of the seams is torn and every day I poke the stuffing back in. It can't be restitched and can't be thrown out, and I get the analogy, really I do. I stop spinning and look at the tear. I touch it, run my fingers down the hard, shiny edge, feeling the indents scratch my finger where the stitching left gouges. In the winter Tim would pre-warm the vinyl with a blanket or a quilt. He always stretched out first, warming a patch and then moving over to make space for me. I grab at the torn bit of fabric and I rip it. It tears down the seam and stops. It won't come off. I pull and tug and scream at it. I pull out the stuffing and throw it to the floor. He's finally, actually, truly gone.

Outside the wind whispers secrets. It doesn't believe me, it doesn't believe that I can say goodbye.

Play

Shaking, I unlock the door. Sundance is not a stranger, he's a friend. We've always had that thing between us, chemistry. Neither of us willing to explore it, before. We smell of the pub. Pubs smell different these days, with the smokers always outside, but the beer smell is there. Stale and yeasty. It's a heady smell made worse by his breathing behind me. I want to run. Instead I unlock the door and my arm invites him in.

In the kitchen I pour wine from a bottle that was left half-empty in the fridge. It's old, but I've got beer tastebuds now. Sundance takes the glass and clinks mine. I wave him into the lounge and throw a blanket over the tear before we sit. Awkwardness is everywhere.

'Music?' Sundance asks.

I shake my head. There is no music now that doesn't conjure Tim. Even in the music he hates, even in a Top 40 hit or a doof-doof dance track, I can hear his voice, his disparaging voice, analysing, criticising, annihilating any shred of credibility in any music that isn't pure Aussie pub rock'n'roll. With Tim, music featured in every part of our lives. It set the mood, created the feel for whatever we were doing, night or day. Would it be slow and tender, hard and fast, strange and adventurous? There was always a track that suited our mood, and each of those tracks is now a part of my brain that just won't go away, no matter how beer sodden I get.

Sundance nods. I can see he knows enough to regret asking that question.

Without music I don't know what to do. I have nothing to guide me, no script to give me a personality to inhabit. My elbows are pinned to my sides.

The choices we have are to talk about something real – our mutually ruined lives? – or to touch each other. Four hours ago I would have said all I wanted to do was touch another person, just to prove that I could. Now? Not so much.

'I feel awkward, Sundance.'

'Oh, thank God you said that, Alice. So do I. Haven't done this for a while, you know.'

Sundance is a hippie. Tonight he is wearing a hemp shirt and old denim jeans. He is greying and his hair is long and in a scruffy ponytail. Tim would have hated him, called him a cliché because he dresses that way with a day job in the government.

The clock ticks in the kitchen. Counting down the seconds, each one diminishing my determination to break free. Each tick a reminder of the old patterns, a reminder of Tim. A step towards fear. Impulse is my only chance. I lean in and kiss Sundance. His face feels fleshy, Tim's was bony. His lips are full, Tim's were thin. Sundance kisses me back. He lacks the rhythm Tim had, or maybe it's that Sundance and I haven't worked out our rhythm yet. I persist with a mule-like determination. Sundance puts his arms around me and moans. Tim would have whispered a lyric in my ear. Sundance's body presses into mine and the fullness of it is shocking. His arms feel muscular but soft, like he's all there, every part of him, nothing is missing. With Tim, there was always a part of him that he'd shaved off and given away. Each difference is a gift. I am suddenly and surprisingly happy.

FARAJ, CORALIE AND RUBY

Housing Needs Assessment

Housing Needs Assessment: Application
Date: 10/2/2013
Housing Officer: Coralie Dunbar
Client: Faraj Mohammed

Health/Disability Issues: N
Financial Issues: Y
Social/Cultural Issues: Y
Current Tenancy Issues: Y
Exceptional Circumstances: N
Suggested Category: 2

Please provide reasons for Category 2 recommendation.
Client is a 17 y.o. unaccompanied minor and asylum seeker from Afghanistan. He has limited English language skills and is attending high school. He has inadequate financial resources (his income comes from Centrelink) and is unable to secure work.

Client has no security of tenure and faces imminent homelessness. He is currently living with another refugee whose wife is due to arrive soon. When she arrives, the Client will be asked to leave the premises.

Client advised that last month he was kicked out of the house due to deteriorating relationship with the other tenant and was forced to sleep in a park for several nights.

Client has requested individual housing, but the Housing Officer does not see any circumstances which would prevent him from sharing with appropriate persons.

Please explain why Client cannot secure housing in private market.
Client faces discrimination in the private rental market due to his lack of English literacy and lack of rental references.

If there are any other issues, please describe.
The original Housing Assessment Support Letter was provided by City West College, where client is attending high school, and stated that issues included 'extreme sadness, anxiety and depression'.

The Housing Officer therefore concludes that without appropriate safe/secure long-term housing the Client's ability to study and work in Australia will be severely impaired.

Housing Needs Assessment: Response
Date: 15/02/2013
Housing Officer: Coralie Dunbar
Client: Faraj Mohammed
The request for housing has been denied.

Housing Needs Assessment: Addendum to Original Assessment
Date: 28/2/2013
Housing Officer: Coralie Dunbar
Client: Faraj Mohammed

Health/Disability Issues: Y
Financial Issues: Y
Social/Cultural Issues: Y
Current Tenancy Issues: Y
Exceptional Circumstances: N
Suggested Category: 1

Please provide reasons for Category 1 recommendation.
Further to my previous report, new information has been made available to the Housing Officer through an interpreter and also psychologist report. This additional information has caused the Officer to change Mr Mohammed from Category 2 to Category 1.

Through the interpreter, Mr Mohammed has advised that he has endured significant trauma and loss and is experiencing chronic mental health issues as a result. It is imperative for his mental health that he has safe, secure and independent housing. The amended psychology report (attached) attests to this and states that Mr Mohammed's mental health will continue to decline if his housing needs are not met.

The psychology report also shows that Mr Mohammed's ongoing mental health issues are exacerbated by living in a shared house. He is currently incapable of developing relationships due to severe emotional trauma. With continued treatment he may regain his mental health, but under present conditions he finds cohabitating distressing and is not able to develop functional relationships with the people with whom he lives.

Psychology Report

Mr Mohammed's psychologist has provided a further letter of support. An excerpt is below:

'It is my professional opinion that Mr Mohammed's present medical condition precludes him from living with others and that it will be beneficial to his ongoing health if he is housed independently. I have diagnosed Mr Mohammed with chronic post-traumatic stress disorder associated with an event in which his parents and brothers were killed when a bomb exploded in his country of birth, Afghanistan. All four were burned almost beyond recognition, while Mr Mohammed played soccer nearby. Mr Mohammed was required to identify the bodies. He is currently distressed by intrusive memories and nightmares, avoidance/numbing behaviours used to cope with re-experiencing the trauma, sleep disturbance, anger/irritability, impaired concentration, hyper-vigilance, anxiety and depression. His condition is long-term and affects his day-to-day activities and ability to cope. His long term prognosis is unknown and contingent upon his responsiveness to treatment.'

Housing Needs Assessment: Response
Date: 12/03/2013
Housing Officer: Coralie Dunbar
Client: Faraj Mohammed
The request for housing has been denied.

Housing Needs Assessment: Application
Date: 26/03/2013
Housing Officer: Coralie Dunbar
Client: Faraj Mohammed

Health/Disability Issues: Y
Financial Issues: Y
Social/Cultural Issues: Y
Current Tenancy Issues: Y
Exceptional Circumstances: Y
Suggested Category: 1

Please provide reasons for Category 1 recommendation.
Faraj is a beautiful boy. Smooth, brown skin. Tall, strong. He might have been an athlete. He has black wavy hair and he wears it long. It flips over his left eye and he doesn't push it away. He's using it to hide from the world and I'm sure he doesn't know it makes him look like James Dean.

He doesn't speak much English and I don't speak Dari so it's difficult to communicate, but we have developed a series of hand signals that he seems comfortable with. Maybe it's easier than speaking. Words can hold so much pain.

Please explain why Client cannot secure housing in private market.
I want to take him home with me. Perhaps my husband and I can cure him of his fear of loss. My husband, who teaches Middle Eastern cultures at the university, will give him our most comfortable chair, and they will speak (although my husband only knows basic Dari and Faraj only basic English).

The conversation will be notable for its mutual concentration, fascination and respect. My husband will make Faraj warm Milo at night time like he used to do when our children were young.

My husband knows that Faraj means 'relief from bad times' and Faraj will be a relief for us both, a chance to focus our energy on someone who needs us, just like the old days, before we started to look at each other blankly after the evening meal. Even though he's not capable of friendship, he will help us.

But Faraj can't stand to be around people.

If there are any other issues, please describe.
One night I will knock on Faraj's door and open it before he has a chance to respond. I will find him with his sleeve pulled up and a compass in his hand. He will be scratching a criss-cross pattern in the soft skin on the inside of his bicep. There will be splashes of blood drying on his jeans and I will realise why he always insists on washing his own clothes. I will wonder where this starts and if it will ever end.

Housing Needs Assessment: File Management
Date: 26/03/2013
Housing Officer: Coralie Dunbar
Client: Faraj Mohammed
File closed and archived.

The Bay

Tonight is cold, for spring, but the tram is warm. I sit where the sun comes through the window, low and bright. There were no clouds in the day and from this I know it will be a cold night. I can't ride the tram forever and the beach will be cold. The wind comes off the water like it's ice.

At Plane Tree Drive the faces were cold but the bed was warm. Ahmad did not want me. In Kabul we would not have been friends. We would have walked past each other on the street and I would have looked to the ground to avoid his eyes. He might have spat at my shoes. But here, we have something in common. We are Asylum Seekers.

Ahmad talks about Afghanistan every day. But I tell him here no one talks like this and history seems very short. Here, the tribes are different. Football-Team-Coloured tribes. Size-of-Your-House tribes. Cost-of-Your-Car tribes.

But Ahmad and I cannot forget the history that lives in our bones. That history was told to us in dangerous words after dinner, since we were alive. We cannot live in that little flat and pretend our families could be friends.

On the tram it is also better to not look at anyone in the eye. But there is a woman opposite who looks up at me every now and then. I wonder why she's not afraid.

We are nearly at the Bay and I try to remember a place I can go to sleep where the wind won't rush through like the *whoosh* of a bomb. Where the cold won't go into my bones.

The woman is looking at me again as she gathers her shiny handbag and finishes her takeaway coffee. She has dark skin like me, but we don't look alike. She smiles at me and I feel warm for a moment, but then I look away.

The tram stops, right before the beach. Everyone gets off and rushes like they have important things to do, but I just walk to the jetty, slowly.

The jetty is old. Paint and rust hold it together. I stop and watch a seagull swoop for something.

'It's gonna be a cold one.'

I turn and see the woman from the tram, looking at her phone. Her voice is big. High like a whistle but strong like a wall.

I nod. She looks up at me and puts her phone in her bag.

'You sleeping rough?'

I don't know how to answer that.

'The backpack. The hair. You look like you need a shower, mate.'

'Ahmad kicked me out,' I say.

'Who's this Ahmad? What did you do to him?'

I can't answer that either. How do you explain years of ancient history that is not even your story?

'I won't bite, lad. You're shaking like a leaf. What's your name?'

'Faraj,' I say.

'I'm Ruby,' she says.

She holds out a hand to me. I can't take it, but I try to smile. Ruby is still looking at me like I'm a puzzle, but then she looks away and out to sea.

'Love this place. Always come here on my way home from work. Just a few minutes, looking out there, is all I need.'

I look where she is looking. The water goes on forever and the sun is getting low. I shiver, thinking about another night outside.

'Where's your mob?' asks Ruby.

'What is a mob?' I ask.

'A family. A history. Your people. Everyone has a mob.'

I shake my head. Ruby is wrong. My mob are all dead.

Ruby starts talking again, slowly as though she's told this story a thousand times.

'Just because you can't see it, or it isn't in the books, doesn't mean it's not real. My mob, my history, isn't in the books, lad. There's no white-fella history that tells my story. My story is here,' she points to her heart, 'and there,' she points to the water. 'We know our stories. We tell them to each other, so that we remember. Always remember, lad.'

But to remember is to hurt and I want to forget.

JENNIFER AND ALEXANDER

All These Hours

While Ava naps, I sit with a pot of tea, glaring at the canvas. I've taken down the simple horizon I painted last week, and placed it paint-side to the wall. The new canvas stares back at me, empty. Paints crack in their tubs, creating deep crevices of darkening colour.

Painting is impossible today. My brain is stuck in a loop, replaying memories. Obsessed, deranged, I pretend to look for something profound, or some clue to unravel or explain away my mistakes, inadequacies and faults.

What I'm really doing is asking myself for permission.

Act 1

Scene: Dilapidated student house – night, 16 years ago

Jennifer: 19 years old, too tall, and in her try-hard punk phase.

Hair: short, spiky, dyed blue-black.

Eyes: rimmed with black eyeliner which is swept up in a thick arc at the outer corner in an attempt to look like

Siouxsie Sioux from the Banshees.

All of it's war paint, a protective layer, and is nothing like the 'come hither' makeup of other girls her age. Jennifer sees the world with brutal clarity: tough, unfathomable, cruel, indecent. She hides behind a constructed image and skulks away. She wants someone to follow her, and ask her why she's hiding.

No one ever does.

The man Jennifer is in love with, Alexander, is dating one of those Come Hither girls: Kerry.

Alexander: short, Czech, vodka-drinking alpha-male. Or so he appears. Jennifer has known him since they were both six years old, so she can recognise his war paint, just as he can see hers.

It's very inconvenient for Jennifer to be in love with Alexander, after all he's dating Kerry.

Kerry: petite private school girl with perfect skin, perfect diction and unsnagged tights.

Jennifer, Alexander and Come Hither Kerry are at a party. Kerry sits on Alexander's lap and doesn't look too big for him. He loops her long, sleek hair around his finger like it's precious silk. He whispers in her ear and makes her smile.

Colette sees what's going on; she's followed Jennifer's gaze, and she figured it out ages ago, anyway.

Colette: stirrer, manipulative as hell, although she'd never admit it, and Jennifer's best friend.

Colette bundles the group together: Jennifer, Alexander, Kerry, Mike and Simon, and takes them outside for a cone. She might have Jennifer's interests at heart, but her methods are cruel and unusual.

Sitting in the banana lounges in the backyard of some distant friend's house, overlooking the dried out swimming pool, and passing around a cone, Colette starts up The Game.

'Let's play The Game! Jen and Alex Are Perfect For Each Other Except... We haven't done that in ages!'

'Nooo!' Jennifer says, weary and embarrassed.

Lying back in a self-assured, casual pose and with Colette on his lap, Mike says, 'Yes! I'll start. Jen and Alexander are perfect for each other except...he has to stand on a crate to kiss her!'

Mike: Colette's boyfriend, borderline sociopath, gigolo.

Everyone except Alexander, Kerry and Jennifer laughs.

'Don't you mean a ladder!'

That is either seriously amusing, or the weed is really good. Tears begin to run down their faces. Kerry is subdued and sullen. Who can blame her? Colette and the others are being arseholes. Jennifer almost feels sorry for Kerry.

'Jen and Alex would be perfect for each other except they would argue about *everything...all the time*!' says Simon.

Simon: normally very nervous and sweet but tonight rendered childish by overindulgence.

'This game *never* gets tired,' says Alexander. He stands, takes Kerry's hand and walks back inside.

And that is the end of that.

The rest of them drift back inside where the music is loud enough to cause brain contusions and the atmosphere is accented by little corners of smoke. Glasses and bottles are on every surface like a modern art depiction of excessive disarray. Bodies are close, limbs entangled, intimacies on display everywhere. Colette and Mike have found a not-quite-dark corner to be indiscreet in. Alexander and Kerry are nowhere to be seen and Simon is mixing complicated drinks in the kitchen, chatting to a handsome stranger.

Above the music, a door slams and Kerry emerges, teary and puffy but somehow still sophisticated and beautiful. She runs for the front door and in a screech of expensive tyres, she's gone.

Jennifer waits for Alexander to race out after her, but he doesn't. She wanders aimlessly around the unfamiliar house, expecting to find him tearful and bereft and despite it all, wanting to console him. But he's nowhere.

She thinks, *I'm coming down and everything looks stupid and ugly and pointless.* She heads for the backyard to be morbid in private. All that remains in the empty pool are sharp salt stalagmites growing on the little blue tiles, pointing up at the stars. An orb weaver spins a web in the tangled garden. From nowhere a pair of arms fold around her waist, a flop of silky fringe tickles the back of her neck, and Alexander sighs into her ear, 'JenJen, will we ever get it together?'

And in those few words, with Alexander's arms around her and his body pressing into hers, what she hears is: *I choose you. I choose you.*

Jennifer knows she is fooling herself. He is in pain and confused. Kerry has probably told him she's had enough of his stupid friends and their idea of fun.

But. Finally, finally, someone has followed her and it's too much to ignore.

She turns to him and although she doesn't want to, she picks a fight. It's the only way she knows how to talk to Alexander.

'Something tells me you and Kerry have already "got it together", more times than I care to think about. Anyway, it's not the getting together that's the problem, it's the *staying* together.'

In the process of her little speech she's extracted herself from his arms, managed to make herself angry at him, and ruined a perfectly perfect moment that could have turned into a romantic moment.

'Are you deliberately misunderstanding me? Since when is "get it together" a euphemism for sex? And why are we even talking about sex? And Kerry? I was talking about you and me.'

'Clearly not a topic at all related to sex.'

'Clearly.'

What is that she detects in his voice? Bitterness? Distaste? Sadness? Regret? She can't tell.

'So did Kerry finally get sick of us all? I wouldn't blame her if she did.'

'It's not about "us", it's about her and me. It's just not working.'

'You might think it's not about "us", but it is. We are vultures. Carnivorous. Ruthless. Kerry was the weakest link. Only the strongest survive and earn our friendship.'

'You might be right about that,' he sighs.

'Oh, look at that, something we can agree on,' Jennifer says sourly.

'JenJen, why do we do this?'

'Do what?'

'Pick fights with each other.'

'You're fun to fight with. You bite back.'

Alexander takes a step towards her, his hands held up.

'What about a peace offering? I don't want to fight with you tonight.'

Jennifer feels like snarling, *I'm not a replacement! You can't come to me for comfort when your girlfriend walks out on you.*

Instead, she says, 'Peace offering? Exactly what is on the table?'

'Sometimes I want us to be...different...kinder. I care about you, JenJen. Can't we have both? Can't we challenge each other and...I don't know...love each other too?'

Jennifer wants to kiss him right now, there is nothing in the world that matters more. Not a damn thing. This is the grand moment she's been waiting for. *I'm going to do it,* she thinks. She takes a step and hears a sharp gasp from behind Alexander.

Kerry.

Alexander turns to her and drops his arms. Jennifer flees making a much noisier and less stylish exit than Kerry did, in her backfiring Corona.

The sun has set and it's dark in my studio. Hours have passed and I'm still staring at the canvas, only now it's not blank. I've painted Alexander's face. I stand up and put my fingers to the wet paint on his lips, drag them down and smear his chin, which I've painted with exaggerated lines that make his intractability look more like my own. I put my paint-wet fingertips to my lips and send him a kiss.

STEVO

I Go To Rio

The woman sits on the tall stool in front of me and asks for a flight to Rio de Janeiro. I have to look up the airport code: GIG. Won't forget that again.

The brown leather strap of her bag is almost the same colour as her skin, and is the same width as the shoulder of her tank top. She puts her green beaded necklace in her mouth and sucks on it like a nervous child.

'Return?' I ask.

Masses of tight dark brown curls spring out around her face and look like they could never be brushed. They bounce on her bare shoulders, even when she is still. She spits out the necklace so she can speak.

'No. One-way. I'm going home.'

Her eyes flick to the floor before her expression catches up with her words and she remembers to smile.

From the stool she is much higher than me. They do that on purpose – so that the customer feels uncomfortable and doesn't settle in for a chat about bus routes in Cairo or the safety ratings of minor airlines in Russia. It also means the customer is conveniently able to look down their sales consultant's blouse, or directly at their groin, as they prefer.

'Can I have your name and date of birth, please? So that I can start building a quote?'

She gives them to me.

'Contact number? Email?'

She gives them to me.

I have all the Key Information now and she is in our database. We can stalk her with advertising and QuoteBeats.

'Great, thanks, Juliana. I'm Stevo by the way,' I say, pointing to my name tag. 'Do you have a preferred airline?' I use her name, the way I have been trained to, to create a false sense of friendship between us.

'The cheapest.'

She has an accent I find both charming and confounding. It makes me hang onto each syllable to make sure I've deciphered correctly.

'Okay. What date do you want to fly?'

This should be an easy fare. In theory I could add a sizeable commission to the base. But her eyes flick to the carpet every time she speaks and the necklace keeps going in and out of her mouth and it makes me reluctant to rip her off.

I type in ADL–GIG and the date and give her the cheap options: Aerolineas Argentinas and Emirates. I explain to her about the layovers associated with each flight, heavily emphasising the benefits of Emirates – making 23 hours in Dubai into a selling point – because this month we have a deal with them and if I can sell another five Emirates fares I get a free return airfare to any Emirates destination. It's a helluva reward and no one else in my office is even close. I really want that free flight. I want to go to Casablanca, walk into a piano bar and say, 'Play it again, Sam.'

'Dubai? I don't know. That's a lot of extra miles. I'll take the Aerolineas flight. Do you need a deposit now?'

This is the easiest sale I've ever made in the four years I've been doing this job. They *always* try to get you to hold the fare while they shop around and come back to you with a quote they want you to beat.

'You're sure? Dubai is *amazing*! Have you seen the shopping malls and the indoor parks? It's like nothing else on earth!'

Desperation is creeping in. Nothing kills a sale faster than desperation mixed with a sniff of insincerity. It's obvious she doesn't care about shopping malls or indoor parks. I'm an idiot.

She shakes her head, glossy curls bouncing away, and waits for me but the only sentences I seem to be able to form are not appropriate. Why are you so anxious? Have you always sucked on your necklace, since you were a child? Did you need braces for that? What're you going home to? What're you leaving behind? Is there a *who*? Or is it just a *what*?

'Aerolineas, please. Do you need a deposit?' she repeats.

I snap out of it.

'$200 is fine. And the rest within the week. Is that okay?'

'Okay.'

She fishes around in her purse and hands me flat and tidy notes – straight from the ATM – then she's gone before I remember to tell her to bring her passport in.

'What was with that commission? You could have doubled

that, easy,' says Ruby from the desk next to me.

'What?' I say, catching up too late.

'You just blew Casablanca, Stevo,' Ruby shakes her head. In this line of work there is no greater goal than an airline reward. And no greater chump than me.

But Casablanca seems unimportant now. Because I've fallen in love with a girl who's going to Rio and I have five days to sell five more fares. Emirates fly ADL to GIG. The image of Sam sitting at his piano crooning 'As Time Goes By' is replaced in my mind by Peter Allen swinging his maracas as he dances around his grand piano singing 'I Go To Rio.'

I'm going to Rio.

CORALIE AND LEYTON

The Theatre

Driving down Plane Tree Drive, on my way to work in the city, I shut the vents in my car. The pollen from the plane trees, like yellow puffs of fairy floss, has bothered me since I was a child.

Faraj used to live on Plane Tree Drive and I briefly consider an unscheduled visit to try to find out where he is now. Why he couldn't live with his carer, why he wouldn't talk to me, why he vanished, slipping through the cracks of a system gaping with holes. There are a thousand whys I can't answer about him. All my instincts are screaming at me, telling me he needs me. But I know the answers aren't here anymore. And because the Department doesn't know where he is, my instincts can scream all they like, it's no use.

Nearing the corner of South Road, where the theatre is, old memories settle over me. The curl of the purple and green ornamental façade, crumbling at the corners, the doors pushed closed with rain-warped, drafty gaps. The empty billboard. Tunes whisper to me as I come closer, songs long gone and impossible to forget. Days of rehearsal and nights of fevered performance prickle my skin. People tucked close in the crowded backstage, hours of preparation in the green room, giggling leotard-clad girls and mothers fussing over hair and makeup.

The traffic is bad this morning, even on the Drive, and I wonder if I'll be late for work. I mentally check my diary for early appointments as orange cones direct traffic away from the theatre and squash us into one lane.

Sitting in the right lane, creeping forward towards the theatre, I watch a man in a hard hat yell instructions into a walkie-talkie, gesticulating aggressively to someone in a bobcat. Machinery, scaffolding and fences engulf the theatre.

Are they doing it up, or pulling it down?

I feel sick all day. As I talk to clients, I barely register any of it. I go through the motions; grant temporary extensions, book inspections, call Family Services three times, sit on hold forever. I try to retain a veneer of compassion, even though there is so little left in me.

Then Faraj comes in again. I still don't have any housing to offer him. I ask why he can't go back to Ahmad and his dark eyes flick to the floor and stay there. He doesn't answer. I ask him a hundred questions, just to keep him close for a while. I tell myself that while he's with me, at least, he's not being hurt. But who am I kidding? He carries his hurt like a torch. There is no escaping it. And none of the questions I ask change the fact that I can't give him what he needs. I'm stalling. Hoping to get to the bottom of him. I give him a list of shelters and he takes it, but I know full well he will choose to sleep rough rather than go to one of those places and I don't blame him.

I knock off at five and race through the city, driving recklessly. Pulling up on South Road, I watch from my car. The crane is still. The men in hard hats and bright jackets are gone – all but one. He wears a suit underneath his safety gear. He is looking up at the sky. Imagining what? Ten sterile storeys?

I jump out of the car and dodge the peak hour traffic to cross the road.

'Hey!' I call out.

His gaze drops from the monstrosity in his mind and turns to me.

'Hi.'

'What's going on?' I ask.

'We're tearing it down.'

The words register brutally, as if they are wedging into my brain with a block splitter. I reach out and curl my fingers through the wire fence. The worn and patchy velvet on the chairs, the embellished wallpaper, the ancient splintery floorboards. All gone. The chandelier. Oh, the chandelier.

'Are you okay?' the man asks, obviously sensing an old duck like me might pass out any second of the day, forcing him to write up an incident report.

I ignore him and walk back to my car.

Sleep doesn't come easily. I spend half the night fending off my husband's knees and elbows. Eventually I fall into a dreamless torpor that is broken by the canaries. They don't care that it's the weekend.

I shower, dress, eat and drive to the theatre.

It's quiet and Plane Tree Drive is deserted. The houses are silent, sitting placidly in the shade of the plane trees. It's still early; the frost is still on the grass. I walk to the stage door and try the gate: bolted and chained. I return to my car and haul out the heavy bolt cutters. After working in public housing for a lifetime you learn a trick or two. As I try the chain I wonder what will give first – my bones, or the hardened steel – then the lock snaps and I ease the gate open. Signs scream at me to WEAR SAFETY GEAR AT ALL TIMES and REPORT TO THE OFFICE BEFORE ENTRY TO SITE.

The alley behind the theatre is disgusting these days. Sheets of newsprint like urban tumbleweed. Corners used as a urinal and worse. Bits and pieces of shabby lives scattered into a windblown wound. In my sensible shoes, I pick my way through it to get to the stage door.

Not much has been done yet. It looks like they are still setting up the machinations of their destruction. The stage door is unlocked, presumably the locked gates are considered enough protection for the old building, so I walk into the dark corridor that leads to the green room. As a child, I ran these corridors barefoot, leaping and laughing as we practised the routines in any space we could find. Later I brought my own daughter here for her dance concerts.

The green room is a sad place; empty, hollow, cold. It was never decorated gloriously like the rest of the theatre, but had always been filled with the warmth of a hundred bodies and needed nothing more.

I keep walking and find my way onto stage. I am ten

again, dressed in flowing pink tulle and sequins, arms and legs smeared in orange Leg Tan, eyelids electric blue, hair scraped into a painful bun. I spin and stretch; each step is like putting on an old coat. Mum and Dad smile when we take our bow. Their pride glows like lanterns. We scamper off stage, in our excitement forgetting the strict instruction to exit stage left in a tidy line with toes pointed and chins high. That doesn't matter. All that matters are the waiting hugs.

Now, I sit on the boards and wind my arms around my waist, allow myself to be flooded with melancholy. Until a sound disturbs me. A bird, no doubt nesting in the old ruins. The birds will lose their home too. There will be no place for them in this new structure. I briefly consider trying to catch them but my husband won't tolerate any more strays being brought home. And my neighbours already complain about my squawking canaries.

Monday, Monday. It always comes around too fast. I take the quick route to work, unable to bear the thought of being stuck in traffic in front of the theatre as a wall crashes down. But by the end of the day my curiosity, and many years of habit, get the better of me.

The man is there again, looking up at the sky. Again. Either he has very little imagination or he is trying to predict the weather. I walk up to the fence and clutch the cold wire.

'Hi,' he says.

'Hi.'

'It's going to be beautiful. They're calling it Theatre Apartments and there'll be a monument.'

I scoff. 'Huh!'

He looks at me closer.

'Do you know this place?'

'Better than you do if you think anything else could be more beautiful.'

'But it's crumbling. It's dangerous. No one uses it anymore,' he says.

'You don't throw things away because they are crumbling. You nurture things that aren't strong,' I say.

He pauses for a while, trying to understand. I can see he wants to. But he can't. He lives in a world where things that aren't perfect are replaced. He's so young.

'I'm Leyton,' he says.

'Coralie,' I say as I walk away.

'See you!' he calls out.

I make it a habit. I drive the long way to work to make it easier to get through my day, and on the way home I go and see what layer they've torn down. Elements are thrown into bins to be reused or dumped. At least some of it will be recycled. The floorboards will be sanded and oiled and used to fancy-up some run-down eastern suburbs mansion. The glass doors might be used by someone wanting to add character to their severe modern home. The ragged red velvet curtain will be dumped.

The man isn't looking at the sky today. He is smiling at me.

'I have something for you,' he says.

He strides towards a pile of rubble at the back of the site.

'Come to the side gate,' he says. 'I'll let you in. You don't need your bolt cutters this time,' he winks.

He unlocks the new padlock, opens the gate, slips a fluoro jacket over my suit and puts a hard hat on my head.

'Sorry, I'll be fired if you don't wear it.'

He is still smiling his goofy smile.

'This way,' he says.

We walk through the front doors, now just empty frames.

'Watch your step,' he says.

'Okay,' I say, thinking that I couldn't fall in this place in a million years; I know it too well. But he's right. The floor isn't there anymore – just struts and dull, tired dirt remain. I pick my way over it and follow him to the foyer.

'I found this.'

He is shy now. His offering in his large, rough hands, held out to me.

'I don't know what it is, but it looked beautiful. I wanted… to save it.'

He holds a small brass fixture, newly polished. I don't know exactly what it is either, or where it came from. I take it and its chill shivers through me.

'Thank you,' I say. It is an unknown piece of me, given back to me by this unknown man, and I am overwhelmed.

'I didn't want it to end up in a salvage shop. Don't ask me why,' he laughs nervously.

I smile at him and notice something different about his face that I can't quite register.

Leyton and I talk every day; he tells me what they've done. It seems peculiar to me that so much care is taken to destroy something. They could have just put a bomb under it. But as it turned out, the theatre is still a valuable commodity.

In pieces anyway. Famous light fittings and rows of seats are to be sold at auction. Apparently there are people, past performers and patrons, who want to hold onto it more in its demise than its life.

One day Leyton comes to the fence with a look of sadness I've never seen before. Normally he is so invigorated by his work.

'What is it?' I ask.

'Coralie, tomorrow they blast whatever's left. I've grown quite attached to the place,' he laughs his nervous laugh. 'Do you want to come in? One last time?'

I do, I do. But. It will make it harder to walk away.

'No.' I say.

He looks like I've slapped him.

'Please come in. I want to show you something.'

I sigh and follow him in. As we pick our way through the rubble I say, 'We're all growing old, after all. I guess this will be your fate eventually, too.'

I'm talking to his back, but I see his steps slow. He doesn't speak 'til we reach the stalls.

'I'm supposed to have disconnected this by now... Wait here.'

He runs off to the back of the room and flicks a switch.

The darkness is obliterated and the theatre is washed in the crystal glow of the chandelier. Shadows are cast in patches but it is impossible not to see the place has been gutted and tortured.

Still, with the graceful light of the chandelier it seems almost unspoilt.

'They can't get it down. We've had experts come in from

all over. They want to save it of course, it's worth a mint. Tomorrow we'll take it down with the crane and hope for the best. Weighs a tonne.'

The songs return to me like an echo. 'The Good Ship Lollypop' when I was just five. 'Thriller' when my daughter was twelve – her last performance before puberty got the better of her. Dozens in between. They course through me, wave upon wave. Applause. The acrid smell of Leg Tan and hairspray. Cheeks sore from smiling. Mum's perfume when she hugged me, forgetting or not caring that I was covered in orange goo. Dad mimicking the steps in a hilarious melange, laughing as he tripped and stumbled. My senses drown me.

'I know it sounds crazy but I like it in here at night. I hear things I can't explain. Like it's alive. That's why I'm always here when you come by,' he says.

'It was never alive, it was the people that made it come to life.'

He walks back and stands next to me.

I reach out and take his rough, young hand.

JENNIFER AND AVA

Milk Cup

'Ava, when you ask for something, use your Mighty Girl Voice, not your Mouse Voice,' I say.

Ava is talking lots now, but when she asks for something it is in such a quiet voice that I have to strain and lean in to hear her.

'Milk please, Mumma,' she repeats. Her voice is still so small that I can barely understand.

'I can't hear you, darling. Speak up. Remember, Mighty Girl Voice. You are a Mighty Girl!' I put one hand on my hip and the other, fist clenched, I raise to the ceiling.

She looks at me like I'm a bit mad.

I sigh and pass her the milk cup.

FLORENCE, DOUG, GLORIA AND NEVILLE

Kind of Blue

A large rectangular leather box is beside me. The yellowed stitching is fraying and it reminds me of Florence's dress. Birds the colour of an overcast sky swoop at my car windshield. People in small swimming clothes sit under colourful rain sticks on the sand.

I open the leather box. Inside is an instrument I can play but not name. I take it out and put it to my lips. My fingers twitch in patterns, up and down, up and down. There is something old in them. I perfect my embouchure and blow. Fingers go up and down, up and down. The overcast birds stop attacking my car and fly away. Tasteless critters don't like jazz.

Every note from *Kind of Blue* comes to me like a gift but I can't remember how to get home. I throw the useless instrument onto the passenger seat. My empty hands are blotchy, papery and crumpled. Nails yellow, too long and brittle. These hands have their own knowledge aside from my pitiful brain; of jazz and blues and a woman called Florence.

I get out of the car and walk to the sand. It's hot and there are people everywhere. I go from towel to towel, looking under the rain sticks.

'Florence! *Flossy*!' I yell.

Children see me and cry.

We got married on a day like this. Florence wore blue and looked like the sky. We danced for hours to Miles Davis.

She is not here.

In 1959 Florence's blue dress had tiny fabric-covered buttons from her neck to the floor. My fat but nimble fingers undid each of them: she became my symphony. An azure butterfly, her dress floated to the floor. I imagined her naked belly swelling with the babies we wanted and time stopped.

So much has been taken.

Stitches

I've cut up Doug's sausages, mashed his potato with butter and dried chives, and cooked the peas and carrots until they are too soft. Our little dining room is dark now; the mottled pink Formica table is half in shadow.

As always, when Doug is late, I fret. Why didn't I put my foot down about the driving? The problem's not the forgetting, it's how the forgetting makes him feel.

Car wheels crunch the gravel in the driveway and my skin tightens.

He curses as he fumbles with his keys. I scuttle to the door as fast as these old legs will go and let him in.

'Hello, dear. How did it go?'

'Do you think I can't open my own front door, woman?'

He slings his trumpet to the floor. It hits the side table and dents the wall. I follow him to the bedroom.

'Are you hungry?'

'I let them down again. A three-piece with two players.'

'Doug, they understand.'

His face constricts and releases like a contorted heart at the word 'understand' and his eyes burn at me.

Of all the changes, the carelessness with which he treats his trumpet surprises me the most. It had been his third arm, his great love, not to mention his income, for over fifty years. There was a time when he treated it as though it was as delicate as fairy floss. There was a time he treated me that way too. He used to call me My Fragile Flossy, and I let him do it because we both knew it was ironic.

I pick up the instrument and put it in the cupboard. On the carpet there's a small chip of paint from the wall. Another fracture, another token to collect.

Back at the bedroom, the door is closed.

'Shall I put your dinner in the microwave?' I ask through the door.

Doug pulls the door open, pushes me aside and strides to the kitchen. He picks up the plate and throws it at the wall. Mash splatters and sausage slides. Peas roll and carrots drop. The plate is melamine. I've learned not to use china.

He shoves me against the wall too, my scapulas press and feet slip. He pushes his forearm across my throat, the skin-sheathed bone of his arm juts into my windpipe. He stares at me like he doesn't know who I am, then releases me and walks away.

Shaking, I clean up his mess.

In bed, sleep doesn't come for a long time. Then Doug is on top of me and his weight forces the air from my lungs.

'Doug, stop, please,' I beg.

Doug's body is old and frail, his muscles long depleted, but so are mine. He grabs my shoulders and violence contorts his face. I don't like to use the word rape, but there is no other word for it, even though he is my husband and he is so very unwell.

When Doug is finished with me he sits on the edge of the bed. He takes the glass of water from the bedside table, has a sip, then smashes the glass on the bedhead. This is new and my heart gives a jagged flutter. His hand is cut and droplets of blood fall onto the quilt cover, mixing to pink in the spilt water.

He studies the broken glass in his hand and even his blood seems slow to come, melancholy. Sitting up, a piece of glass pierces the palm of my hand.

Doug's bleeding doesn't stop so I find the antiseptic and bandaids. When I get back, he hasn't moved. I gently dab his cuts. He flinches, but remains impassive. The bandaids will rupture his old skin when they have to be peeled off, but those cuts won't heal on their own.

'I don't think you'll need stitches,' I say. 'Let's go back to sleep. We're going to the Barossa tomorrow, remember?'

The word 'remember' is a mistake.

Flossy

It was an invitation we couldn't turn down; there was a need in Gloria's phone call. That's the irony of old age: it brings back the urgency of youth. Gloria is dying.

When we were young, Doug would drive with one hand resting casually on the wheel, his elbow poking out of the open window. The other hand would rest not so casually on my thigh. Country drives – the silences that didn't need to be filled, and the depth of the land that defied explanation – used to be a comfortable part of our lives. Now they're another lost thing.

Doug looked out the window as I drove.

'Not far now,' I said.

Doug grunted in reply and a few more kilometres went by quietly until he finally spoke.

'Look at that water-nest,' he said. 'Hasn't seen the rain for a while.'

I looked at the dam Doug was pointing to, a muddy indent in the rolling green hills, and thought, *what a pretty thing to call it.*

Back home after our trip to the Barossa, I change the quilt cover. The dry blood looks like impressionist blossoms before I rip the sheets off the bed.

That night I dream a distant memory.

I am cuddling Eldon, our youngest child, on my knee. He has his fingers in his ears. The girls are built for this life, but Eldon doesn't like the noise and bustle of his dad's gigs. He is the black sheep in a way, a loner in a family of gregarious people. But Doug, the girls and I adore him for it; we love him excessively and almost competitively.

The girls are dancing in front. I smile as I watch them. In the dream, with Eldon on my knee, I'm conscious of wondering what will become of them all.

Doug is watching the girls dance as he plays. It's hard to smile and play the trumpet, but it sneaks up to his eyes.

The set is over, not soon enough for Eldon, and Doug tucks his girls under his arms and walks over to the table where Eldon and I sit. He waves to the barman – lemonade all round. Doug takes Eldon onto his lap so that I can get the circulation back in my legs. Eldon smiles at his father, a man he loves but doesn't understand.

'How about we go to the beach tomorrow?' Doug asks us all.

'Yay!' sing the kids. The girls do a little jig.

Tomorrow is a school day, and bursting the bubble will make me the bad guy. The idea will be forgotten by morning anyway.

I wake to the phone ringing and the dream is gone.

'Hello?'

'Mum, it's me.'

'Oh, hi Eldon.'

'You sound shaky. Are you okay?'

'Yes I'm fine, just woke up. How are you?' I make an effort to control my voice.

'Sorry, Mum, I forget you don't have a 6am live-in alarm clock. How's Dad?'

'Not good, Eldon. I think,' I lower my voice, 'I think we need to contact the nursing home.'

'Mum, come on. He just forgets, you can't lock him up for that.'

'It's not locking him up, Eldon. They can care for him better than I can.'

'Can't we just let him enjoy the time he has left?'

I recognise my granddaughter's mournful wail in the background. Mia, who is just learning to walk, probably fell over.

'You go look after Mia, Eldon. I'll speak to you later.'

I hang up the phone and close my eyes. I am still protecting my children.

'Flossy? Flossy? Are you there?' Doug calls from the bedroom.

My skin tightens.

He finds me and puts his arms around my waist, nuzzling me like a kitten.

'There you are,' he says.

Gloria

In '55, all we wanted was freedom in love. Do you remember what we said, darling Florence? 'Freedom in love is the condition for all other freedoms.' We weren't free to love more than one man. A black man? Forget it! A woman, of any colour? No way. We weren't free to join the blokes in the public house. How dull life was! Corsets and curlers. No wonder we did what we did. You and I were never meant to be *Women's Weekly* housewives, but anarchy didn't suit us either. 'The desire for security and sufficiency is the very mark of the servile mentality.' Boy. Fighting words! And fight we did.

Despite all that, I did love just one man, as did you. It was enough, wasn't it? But we needed to know that it would be, didn't we? We needed to choose. Anarchy turned out to be overrated, but I'm glad I gave it a darn good shot.

Nearly sixty years later, my dear friend, and I still love Neville, and you Doug. But here we are, in the 'twilight of our lives', as my silly daughter says. Twilight? Twilight implies a gentle setting sun, softening everything. What could be more wrong? There is nothing soft about dying. No light can hide the wrinkles on my skin. And cancer is like a stubborn bastard of a boulder, not a setting sun. There is nothing subtle about the way our bodies and minds fail us, one creak or crack at a time.

On your visit last week, my dear, you looked worse than me. *You* are not dying, you're strong as an ox and always were. So what is it, Florence? You wouldn't talk to me on Sunday. I wish we were twenty again and nothing in our lives was secret from the other. I wish I could pretend we were still sharing that flat we had in teacher's college and it was the end of a long night with our fellas and we were sitting on our lumpy beds gossiping about men.

But we don't have to do that, really. I can guess.

From: Gloria West
To: Florence Freedman
Subject: Libertarianism

Dear Florence

Doug is getting worse and you can no longer manage it. I know we don't talk about this, especially not in front of Douglas, but I might be dead next week.

My dear, don't wait 'til it's too late. You are too utterly precious. Go back to 1955 and remember what it felt like to value yourself more than you valued society's rules, and bugger anyone to hell if they stand in your way.

Neville is growling at me to stop on the computer. He wants me to lie down and die but I refuse.

Gloria

From: Florence Freedman
To: Gloria West
Subject: Libertarianism

Dear Gloria

It turns out I did love two men, but not the way we imagined back then. This disease has split Doug in half and somehow I do love them both because I can see them meeting in the middle from time to time. There is a glimpse of one always in the other. How can I send one away, knowing he takes the other with him?

Lie down, but don't die. I'm coming to see you. On my own this time.

Florence

Morphine

Eldon arrives to look after Doug and I get in the car and drive like a bat out of hell. I hope Doug will have a bad day so that Eldon will see what I can't tell him. I refuse to feel bad about having that thought.

It's lovely in the Barossa today. The sun reflects off the golden hills on one side of the road, and lights up the iridescent green of the vines on the other. The earth is brittle and plush, all at once.

Neville answers the door, his face bleak.

'I didn't give her the full dose of morphine, Florence. She wanted to be able to talk to you. But she won't last long like that.'

I thank him and go to Gloria's room.

In just a week she has stepped closer to the edge of life than seems possible. I hold her hand and she opens her eyes. She is a skeleton held together by skin-coloured tissue paper. I do not cry when she tries to squeeze my hand, but I can no longer remember how I got here. It doesn't matter. We look at each other and that's all.

Neville comes into the room and takes Gloria's other hand. It is a silent vigil and with Doug missing it is incomplete, as my life will always be from now on.

Then Gloria is gone.

There is no drama. Her breath is there, and then it's not.

I say a small prayer to a god I don't believe in, begging for her to be looked after.

'Most of all, I will miss her wickedness,' Neville says trying to smile through his tears.

'Me too,' I say. But it's not quite true. Most of all I will miss her counsel when the time comes, soon, and I must be braver than I feel.

JENNIFER AND BROCK

Retreat

I dreamt about Alexander and woke feeling peaceful, but when Ava cries from her cot, hungry and wet, my peace ruptures. I am falling into the gaps in my life and the gaps are getting bigger.

I have signed up to go away with fifteen strangers for three days and do nothing but paint. I told Dan that I need to rebuild my sense of self, that I am lost in nappies and sleep deprivation and I need to be away from it all for a while, and to focus on something challenging, something creative. With something that I took for understanding in his eyes, Dan agreed without hesitation. He cares enough to want me to be better. He said, 'Whatever you need, darling,' and took the Friday off work to be home with Ava. I'm sure I detect relief that I'll be gone.

The retreat is in a bushland setting, and damn it all, there are trees everywhere, crowding up to the little barracks that we sleep and eat in. It's supposed to be cosy, but it takes me straight back to the Drive, where the trees are like bars on my cell. I want to see the horizon, paint the horizon. When I suggest this to the instructor, a red-head called Maureen, she laughs and tells me, 'I've seen your horizons, Jennifer. You need to challenge yourself. Paint a tree for a change!' She's right of course, but that doesn't mean I have to like it.

In groups of four we are sent into the bush to choose a small detail of some kind and paint it. The plan is that we compare the four visions of the same object and examine how four people can create something so different from a single object.

Brock and I paint the burrow in the same terms. Our brush strokes are almost identical, the colours we choose cannot be told apart and the burrow looks as though it was painted by the same person. We share the same inability to see beyond the burrow and into its abstract nature. We are literalists. I feel certain that we see the world through the same lens and that we will have the most fascinating conversations. I feel completely exposed.

That's when I notice: I'm *feeling* something other than fatigue and boredom and guilt.

That night Brock and I sit in front of the radiator with Maureen and the rest of the group, scrambling for heat like we're on power rations, stomping our feet quietly to keep the blood flowing. Brock and I steal glances and smiles. I feel raw. My toes are tingling, the floor underneath them unstable and crumbling away with each stomp.

Talking to the group, Brock is earnest, restrained and intelligent. I can see him holding back when someone in the group says something patently stupid. There is something else I see in him. It's something I saw in Alexander – he's constantly *constructing* himself, proving himself to the world. With Alexander it was his foreignness that made him scared of himself. I don't know what it is with Brock, but I see it in him too. He's presenting the Brock Who Is Acceptable To This Group Of People. It makes me want to deconstruct him, shake him up, the way I wanted to shake Alexander up when I used to pick fights with him.

These thoughts are hazardous. I get up and walk to the kitchen. As the kettle boils a voice comes from behind me. Someone has followed me. I turn around.

'What do you make of that "four painters four burrows" business?' Brock says.

'It's nonsense. We like to think we are incredibly unique, but in fact our brains are pretty much hardwired by convention by the time we are three or four,' I say. Brock is leaning on the kitchen bench that is between us.

The kettle boils and I pour my cup of tea, holding the kettle up to Brock in a question. He puts his cup down and plonks a tea bag in it. I pour.

'And here I was thinking you and I were cosmically bound by mirrored thought patterns or something. But really we were just being conventional. Buzz kill,' Brock smiles.

'Yep, that's what they call me. Buzz Kill Jennifer.'

I hold out my hand, a formal introduction. He takes it and we shake. We don't let go. He holds my eyes and my hand and I feel perilously exposed.

'It is a pleasure to meet you, Buzz Kill, and to finally find another person whose brain and brush understands my own brain and brush. I've been accused of being too literal, you know. Of not looking beyond the object and into its essence, but that's just bollocks. The object *is* its essence, don't you think?'

We are still holding hands.

'So you're not a surrealist, I take it?'

Brock laughs – throaty, deep, gruff.

He looks at my hand, turns it over.

'You don't have painters callouses. Or paint under your nails. Are you a fraud, Buzz Kill?'

'Afraid so. I'm a filmmaker. Painting is...stress relief.'

I like how my hand feels in his. His examination of my skin is gentle, mostly done with his eyes. He traces lines with his left hand, which I notice does not have a wedding ring. His fingers find *my* wedding ring, a thin band of gold with a small diamond, and trace that too, then he lets my hand go.

I notice his hands are deeply stained.

'You're no fraud, that's for sure,' I say. 'Do you ever wonder what it's like to be totally free? Not to be concerned with convention or social rules. Just to be.'

'No, I don't wonder. You've just described my life from the age of fourteen to about...oh, last year.'

It makes sense now, the construction I saw as Brock talked to the group. He is creating himself, building himself up from the rubble of some kind of life.

'What happened last year?'

'I decided it was time to grow up.'

'I've been grown up my whole life. Trust me, it's too hard and it's overrated,' I say.

'Yes, it is. I'm discovering that's true.'

'I could do with a little grown-down for a change,' I say.

'Grown-down? That's a thing?'

'Yeah, it's what adults do when they are sick of rules and responsibility.'

Brock leans forward and takes both my hands and this time I know we are approaching a line.

'I like the sound of that. Feel like being grown-down with me?'

Every sensation hits like I've been given a new body, one that's never felt anything before, one that's never been touched, never been hurt, and never been loved. None of this belongs to me. He flattens my fingers between his two hands so that there is no space between where we touch and where we don't. He curls his fingers through mine. It is soft and careful.

I shut my eyes and when I look again, Brock's question still hangs between us, papering his eyes. There are only two possible answers. He takes my wrist, where I have a small tattoo of a hummingbird that reminds me of being free, and when he kisses it, he snaps the last part of me that's holding onto the reigns of my life. I'd never noticed before how intimate the inside of a wrist could feel.

Brock is untying me.

From around the radiator in the next room we hear the others rise and chairs scrape as they say their goodnights and go to bed. It's been a long day of hard work, where we have all been eager to achieve more than we would normally achieve in a week, keen to prove that we are serious about our work, that the people who are waiting for us back home did not sacrifice their time with us for nothing. We are exhausted with the effort of proving that we are more than the sum of the parts of our daily lives.

We wait for the commotion next door to die down and skip our eyes across the room. My attention is on everything *else*.

Finally there is silence from the other room and we are alone. I nervously reach for my tea cup. Words are beginning to congeal in my mouth and the spell is broken. He searches me for eye contact, which I avoid. He takes my hand, fiddles with my wedding ring, and says, 'See you tomorrow, Buzz Kill,' before walking out of the kitchen.

In bed, I curl into the unfamiliar sheets and try to get comfortable on the too-soft pillow. Restless, I pick up the book that I brought, *Tender is the Night*. I read until Fitzgerald's words swim on the page and my brain gets stuck on a sentence and won't read any further: 'I don't ask you to love me always like this, but I ask you to remember. Somewhere inside of me there will always be the person I am tonight.'

Somewhere inside of me will always be the person who loves a man she cannot have, who time and circumstance and fear, mostly fear, conspired against.

BRUCE

Lottery

Wednesday: I put on my rain jacket and slip off my leather Florsheim work shoes in favour of my waterproof boots and drive to the newsagent.

She greets me the same way each time. Hello Bruce. How's the rain? How's the sun? How's the wind? We never have anything more to say to each other. It's always the same girl. I feel her contempt, she acknowledges mine with her paperback smile. She takes my eight seventy-five, chucks it in the till and runs the machine. One of these days it will spit something decent out. She hands me the ticket and I take it without smiling. I feel her eyes follow me, and it's still raining, bugger it, and I step into a Goddamn puddle the second I walk through the door. I look back at the girl, still watching me and I scowl. 'Fix this damn footpath!' I yell to no one in particular.

She looks back at her counter and starts straightening magazines.

My rain jacket is slick when I get back to the car and

sitting in my bucket seat makes it wet too. I just cleaned it last week. Another pointless task I'll have to repeat for no decent reason.

At home, I stick to my routine and attach the ticket to the fridge in exactly the same spot with the same Gold Coast magnet – the one with a sun-filled beach scene that my sister gave me when she came back from a holiday. Funny the way my brain works, because every time I stick that damn ticket up, on Wednesday and Saturday, I always wonder to myself if I should change my routine, because clearly, it's not bringing me any luck. But I never do. I'm not superstitious. I know it's all out of my control.

I don't cook dinner on Wednesdays. I eat toast and baked beans, imagining it's my last meal in this life. I sprinkle grated cheese and cracked pepper over the beans to make it seem more interesting (sometimes I try barbecue flavour instead) and I sit in front of the TV waiting for the two-minute interval in some crappy show that will give me the magic numbers. A bottle of beer is waiting by my side, but I won't crack it until I win. I change the bottle each year, to make sure it's fresh. Can't imagine anything worse than finally winning this bloody lottery and drinking stale beer to celebrate. If it was Saturday, I'd be sitting there with the real estate pages too, planning the mansion I would buy when I could finally afford to leave this shitty street.

Of course I don't win.

At work the next day I know that if I'd won I wouldn't be at this job that I hate, talking to people I can't seem to get along with and feeling my blood pressure rise with each hour that passes.

They tease me every Thursday morning.

'Pity, Bruce. I'd hoped we wouldn't see you in today.'

Cheryl says this with a nasty edge and a false smile. I know she's pretending to make a joke. I know what she really thinks, too.

'Baz, maybe Saturday, hey mate?'

I hate Darren for calling me Baz like I'm some sort of brickie out on the tools, but at least he's not nasty.

'Wonder who got it this time? Wonder what they're gonna do with it?' Darren says.

'They're not at work, that's for bloody sure,' I say, as I make my way to my cubicle.

I turn on my computer and stare at the screen as the black zaps to Microsoft blue and then the icons pop pop pop like numbers dropping into an electronic barrel.

Emails file into my inbox and Cheryl throws my mail onto my desk.

I think about saying thank you to her and decide against it.

Each email is a problem I have to fix. Me. No one else. And none of them are fixable. This is my job description: fix this, sort that, but don't forget your hands are tied behind your back.

Most nights I'm there 'til eight or later; it's only on Wednesdays that I go home on time, so that I can settle in for the draw. That means on Thursday mornings there is always an unusually high stack of problems to sort through.

I pick through the emails, choosing the problems that have some small hope of being resolved and putting them aside. I look at the demands that will never be fixed and I reply to them. Sorry, read your contract. My hands are tied.

I get up for coffee, returning the silent half smiles of my colleagues as we hover around the coffee machine like the twitchy addicts that we are. Finally, it's my turn at the hissing machine and I take my drink back to my desk to think about the energy expended/outcome returned trade-off of trying to fix those problems that might not be fixable after all.

When Saturday comes around I go to the newsagent again and have the same conversation I always have with the young girl. The Saturday girl is a little less obvious in her condescension than the Wednesday girl. She occasionally asks me how my day is going. 'Don't know yet,' I always reply.

Once I asked her a personal question. What do you do when you're not working here? I saw the disgust cross her smooth-skinned face as she tried to decide whether I was about to ask her out. She realised I wasn't – of course – and told me she studied. Economics.

I never asked her a personal question again, although I always want to, just to see that awful expression cross her face and make her ugly for a moment.

Today she seems to be in a good mood and she asks me about my day.

I wave the ticket she's just given me in the air and tell her she'll know by next week.

A thought shadows her eyes for a moment as she tries to decide whether to say what's really on her mind.

'You know if you saved the money you spent on tickets each Saturday you'd be better off. Because in ten years you still wouldn't have won,' she whispers.

'And Wednesday,' I say absently.

'I shouldn't be telling you this, you're a customer after all. But you know...'

I look at the ticket and know she's right. I'm not stupid. I went to university too. I get paid well above the average. On paper, my life is good – it's just that living it isn't.

I put the ticket in my pocket.

'See you next week,' I say, and walk out of the shop.

I get to the footpath and change my mind. I turn around and walk back to her.

'It's hope,' I say. 'A small price to pay for a little bit of hope.'

Maybe one day she will understand.

HAL, GLADYS AND JENNIFER

How's Your Roof?

I don't bother to clean the window sills, although Evelyn always did. If anyone ever came here these days, it might be different. Visitors, I imagine, give you motivation.

But now there's a knock on the door and I have to make a decision: let them leave, or let them in. What if I open the door and see the recoil on his/her face when they see that I'm the worst kind of lonely?

The knock comes again. I don't have any friends anymore – dead, the lot of them, mostly in the war. I scan the room and realise it's futile. There is nothing I can do to fix it up for guests. I smooth down the t-shirt I'm wearing over saggy grey tracksuit pants and slippers and open the door.

The face smiles at me. He is well-dressed. Hair slicked back with some sort of gunk. His suit is clean and his tie is straight. He's a hundred years younger than me and I can tell this is his first job. He has a freshness about him that will evaporate with time.

'Hello, Sir. How are you today?'

His voice is so bright it's like tulips.

There is one pimple on his left cheekbone. His only physical imperfection, and it's temporary.

I don't answer him, I've forgotten the protocol.

'Ah, well, I'm Rory. I see that your roof needs a bit of TLC, Sir.'

I look around behind me searching the room for the mysterious Sir he's referring to. Of course, he means me.

'Name's Hal, not Sir. Yes, yes it does. Would you like to come in?'

'Thanks, Hal.' He looks into the room behind me. Senses the shambles. 'We can do this right here, Hal, no need to put yourself out.'

My eyes narrow into cat-slits. What would Mitzy do now, if she were still here? Turn away in disdain or give him a warning blow, a slight scratch and a meow?

'I need to sit. These old legs, you know.'

I walk back towards the loungeroom and he follows.

'Sit down, Rory. I'm sorry about the mess. I wasn't expecting visitors.'

I move a pile of papers to make space on the couch and see Rory hold his breath as a smell wafts in his direction.

'Hal, I'm here as a representative of Sheridan's Roofing, we are a local business, no gimmicks. I noticed that the capping on your roof is cracked. And several tiles are also cracked. There is a disturbing slump in the middle of the south-facing pitch that might indicate structural problems. We have a special on at the moment. If you have your roof restored or replaced this month we will throw in a flat screen.'

'A flat screen?'

'A TV. Fifty inch screen! Digital, remote control. You wouldn't have to leave your couch and you'd have access to all the free to air digital channels, right here in your own home. And no worries when it rains, you'll be snug as a bug in here.'

I have to admit he's got me pegged: he's sniffed out my loneliness, my desperation for company *and* my desire to never leave this house again. Maybe he's not as green as I thought. Or maybe he got lucky with me – perhaps that's his sales pitch at every house.

'I'm listening.'

'Well, Hal, all I have to do is get your signature today – just to authorise us into your roof to get a quote, no obligation – and you're on your way. Is next Tuesday okay for the boys to come along and measure up?'

He holds out a single sheet of paper with the word 'Agreement' in bold on the top. I see some future in this. I can drag this out, maybe get 'the boys' here next week, and then the lad back again the week after to explain some misunderstanding with the terms and conditions, and then ask for the manager to come along to inspect a troublesome issue. The next thing you know, I've got People In My Life. Conversations to be had. No more looking out the window watching for the postie to pass me by. No more imaginary conversations with a cat that died fifteen years ago. No more looking at Evelyn's urn on the mantle wishing and wishing that she hadn't died too.

I sign.

'And if you make a successful referral,' Rory says, 'we can give you a discount too!'.

He grins, his teeth as white as icebergs.

The Support Group

I pull my chair in tighter and lean over the Formica-covered table. My hearing hasn't been any good since 1945. I squint at Jennifer, trying to follow the movement of her lips with my rheumy eyes, but those eyes haven't been any good since 1998, and the lighting is bad in Gladys' house.

There is a respectful hush over the room. I only came here because Rory said I'd get a discount if I refer a friend, so I figured I'd better get some. When I arrived, Gladys gave me the rundown on everyone in the room. She told me that Jennifer has sat there more or less mute for six months, listening to everyone else. I wonder why she comes. She's too young for this group of mouldy oldies. But here she is.

The silence in the room has become awkward. Jennifer has been staring at her computer-printed pages for a long time now. People are starting to reposition their sore buttocks on the unforgiving plastic chairs and lean more heavily on their elbows.

Jennifer shakes her head and speaks.

'I'm sorry, I just don't think I'm ready. Maybe next time.'

She looks up and smiles, showing her teeth and doing all the right things, but even with my rotten eyesight, or maybe because of it, I can tell the smile is all on the outside.

Gladys is sitting next to Jennifer. She puts her veiny, thin-skinned hand on Jennifer's, pats it, and says, 'Go on dear, you can do it. We are all friends here. It's time.'

Gladys catches Jennifer's eyes and holds them firmly. She is a formidable woman who has raised children, nursed soldiers during the war and was born in the shadow of the Great Depression. Gladys is all non-negotiable stoicism and expects it from everyone else.

Jennifer nods.

She looks down at the paper and begins to read.

'At first everything went to plan. But plans are made to be broken. Or was that rules? There are no rules for having a baby, and all the plans in the world won't make your hopes come true. Your body has other things in mind for you, the minute you decide to grow another life in it, before it's even conceived, that life has already taken over. By the time my baby was born, he was damaged beyond repair, and so was I. He was ripped from me with bloodied, latex-covered hands, his nerves snapped and torn by the force of the ventouse, forceps and the doctor's hands, as high up on the wall in front of me a TV played the *Big Brother Final Eviction* episode. The worst part of it all took about two hours — I know this because I watched the whole show from beginning to end, and that's what haunts me now. When I hear the theme music to that show I shake, my eyes can't focus, my heart seems to be jumping hurdles in my chest. They call it a PTSD trigger event. Sounds are the worst for me. But the images come too, blood-wet, everything blood-wet and violent. Doctors' calm faces, but with knowing looks between them. Stitching, cleaning, bandaging, the swift cleaning away of human fluids by efficient nurses. All while Christian is evicted from the house for not doing the dishes.'

Jennifer stops at this point. It's clear she hasn't finished, but she can't go on. She's got the shakes. Gladys, next to her, pats her hand again with the knowing look of a woman who's also seen too much blood. And that's when I realise I'm shaking too, and people are looking at me, saying Hal? Hal? in harried voices. I'm clutching the table in front of me, eyes twitching, blood pumping, just like poor Jennifer, and I'm back there with the tanks and the boom of gunfire: the Nazis are coming. There is running and dust and blood and bodies and thundering noise and I can't move.

Now, I fight the urge to cower under Gladys' Formica table, where all those ancient legs are resting like a dormant forest, withered and aged and increasingly useless, just like me. I clutch the table in my bony hands, arthritis preventing me from holding it too tight and I nod my head at them, yes I'm fine, yes, yes. I push the images out first, and then the sounds, just like I've learned to do. Before I knew what this was called, Evelyn used to call it a 'turn'. It was much worse then, in the early days. Of course she didn't sign up for that — night terrors that happened in the days as well, too much drinking, too much sadness, too much violence. No one can bear that and stay whole. Certainly a marriage can't.

Jennifer is bearing into kind Gladys' eyes, matching her rapid breathing to the old lady's slow and steady rate. They are holding hands. Gladys knows, she knows. We have all seen too much of this damn world.

'Do you have a photo?' Gladys asks Jennifer.

Jennifer fishes into her handbag and pulls out her purse, flicks it open and shows Gladys her broken baby, moments before he was gone. Gladys touches his image with her dry fingers. She smiles at the boy and then at Jennifer.

'He's a darling, isn't he?'

Jennifer nods.

But all I can think is that at least that lad will never see war.

MARG, SCARLETT, DENISE AND JEREMIAH

Scarlett's Shed

My daughter visits less and less. There's only so much time I can spend looking at my swimming pool getting brown over winter. And the neighbour's cat swimming in it. I have to admit that, as a distraction, I have become a little obsessed with the World Wide Web. I can find out what's happening anywhere on the planet. War in Syria. Abductions in Africa. Mud slides in Peru. The planet is a mess, quite frankly.

I push the little button with the circle and line and wait for the machine to switch on. Out the window I see Jeremiah dipping his paws into the dirty water.

It would be nice to read something harmless for a change from all this war and terror, so I go to the OnlineShopper website. I leave all the search boxes blank, except for location. There I enter *Plane Tree Drive*. I want to know what's going on in my neighbourhood. Is someone selling baby clothes? Maybe someone wants to buy a bookshelf. Perhaps someone is selling a guitar that has been discarded by an ungrateful teenager.

Two entries come up – one is Jill down the road who is always selling agaves she's propagated from her garden. And the other one is Scarlett's Shed.

Ad placed 6 months ago
Category: Outdoor
Sub Category: Sheds
Sub Category: Other
The shed is made from corrugated iron, Mangrove Colourbond, very discreet, and has a solid iron roof. There are stairs to enter the shed – you must be able to walk to enter.

There is no rust on the panels and there are no holes.

Inside the shed is fully lined with plywood and red velvet wallpaper, providing a warm and sensual feel. The floor is fully carpeted with hard-wearing, easy-clean, commercial-grade carpet.

Fitted with electricity and running water, including a bathroom with spa and double shower. (Please note that you will be asked to shower in the shed prior to services being rendered, towels and soap are supplied.)

The shed is fitted with a king-sized bed and other miscellaneous purpose-built equipment.

Please note that there is a side entrance off Jessie Street and your discretion is essential.

Phone Scarlett for an appointment to view the shed.

Price: $200 p/h (note: **ONO** not accepted, extras charged accordingly)

Location: 21 Plane Tree Drive

Replies

5/8

Mike1968

I'd like to see a picture of the shed before I buy.

5/8

JesseJames69

saw the shed last week. top notch product, but a bit past its prime.

5/8

Stew9999

The latch on the gate sticks. You gotta jiggle it. Could do with some oil.

6/8

BobMcBobby

Is that a euphemism?

6/8

Stew9999

Nah mate.

7/8

BobMcBobby

I took some oil and fixed the gate. Scarlett's happy coz it doesn't bother the neighbours now.

JesseJames69, past its prime? Don't think so mate.

7/8

JesseJames69

i got standards mate.

7/8

BobMcBobby

Yeh, me too mate. And I know a good shed when I see one. Blokes like you don't know your sheds from your shoes.

7/8

Stew9999

McBobby I'm with you. Scarlett's is one of my favourite sheds.

7/8

BobMcBobby

Scarlett's shed is going on holidays. Closed until further notice.

28/11

Stew9999

You can't do that, McBobby. Scarlett, what's going on?

28/11

ScarlettsShed

Scarlett's Shed is still for sale. Business as usual.

28/11

BobMcBobby

Scar, what about Bali? I thought you were coming with me?

28/11

ScarlettsShed

Bob, darlin, what happens in the shed stays in the shed, including the fantasies we act out AND the dreams we talk about after.

SCARLETT'S SHED IS OPEN FOR BUSINESS

28/11

BobMcBobby

Some dreams are bigger than your shed, Scar. I had dreams for us that are bigger than it seems you can imagine.

28/11

ScarlettsShed

ALL DREAMS COME TRUE IN SCARLETT'S SHED. BUSINESS AS USUAL ;)

28/11

TonyTone01

Make my shed dreams come true, 10pm tonight?

28/11

ScarlettsShed

TonyTone01 all bookings by phone, please call me.

I go for a walk. Mercifully, it is a bitterly cold day and there is no one around as I make my way to number 21.

It looks just like any other house. In fact it looks almost the same as mine. Built around the same time, possibly the same builder. The frontage is the same cream brick and I can identify the main bedroom on the left and lounge room on the right, with a corridor down the middle. I can imagine the entire floor plan, even the decor. It could be my house, except that the front yard is a shambles of weeds and rampant couch grass. It's funny that I've never really noticed the house before – it's nonchalant, if a house can have such a demeanour, or any demeanour at all. It looks like it doesn't care what you think of it and dares you to pay it any attention at all. Maybe I'm being fanciful – a house can't have a demeanour. But the curtains are all drawn, silent, like a secret, a cat on the still-warm bonnet of your car in the winter; if it could talk it would say *mind your own business and leave me alone.*

I turn down Jessie Street. The Shed can be seen from Jessie Street, even though the house faces onto the Drive. I can only assume Scarlett had a gate installed on Jessie Street so that her patrons have direct access to the shed and don't need to enter through the house. But Jessie Street, being one of those small utility streets that is all backs-of-houses, has the benefit of anonymity. Residents only end up on Jesse Street once a week, when they put their smelly bins out. I walk up to the gate and examine the lock. It's not been oiled in a while. Dried up grease has attracted grime from the road and gummed up the lock. I feel sad for BobbyMcBobby, his greased latch neglected along with his heart.

It occurs to me that I have the right to feel angry or indignant, but although I can access those emotions as *ideas,* I can't summon them as *feelings.* I find it impossible to care, although there is a small flicker in my heart for poor Bobby taking his trip to the mountains of Bali alone.

I walk back to Plane Tree Drive in time to see a figure

disappear into the front door of Scarlett's house. It has to be Scarlett – all I can see is a tangle of red hair, fluorescent like fireworks, trailing down her back as she passes through the gaudy green door. She's left a grocery bag on the porch and the door reopens, pushed by buttocks, and Scarlett reaches down to pick up the bag. She sees me staring at her. She winks at me, grabs the bag and disappears inside.

That Cat

Denise's house sits at the very top of the street, and from her veranda she has a view into my pool. She must see what her cat does in there. A fence has been built around a huge gum tree that straddles our two properties. The tree allows Denise's overfed cat to roam freely into our yard. The cat, called Jeremiah and named after a bullfrog in a song from a long time ago, refuses to play on the playgym Denise bought for him, refuses to use the run she built for him, refuses to stay in the house at night. He finds a way and quick as lightning, he's out the door. He's a nimble and speedy animal, despite his size.

He refuses to use his litter box, too. Instead he likes to use our pool. He can hold on for days until he has an opportunity.

The tree is heritage listed and cannot be cut down. Never mind that it drops leaves all year round which stain the pool water, making it look like tea. Never mind that the limbs creak and groan murderously and threaten to fall right onto my bedroom roof. Never mind that they give that cat an entry into our yard so that it can defecate in our pool. When she was young, my daughter thought it looked like Tim Tams floating in tea and wanted to know if she could eat one. 'Tim Tam slam!' she said as she reached into the water.

Never mind.

'The cat has to go,' I say to my husband, Martin.

'Yes, yes, but what can we do about it, Marg?'

'Plenty. Leave out poisoned meat. Set a trap. Plenty.'

After years of cleaning cat crap out of my pool, I've quelled any notions of animal rights.

'Can't we complain that it's killing local fauna or something? Get the council to put it down?'

'I don't think the law allows that,' Martin says.

'Well it should.'

'Yes, yes. It should.'

Jeremiah, fat as a bullfrog, likes to swim. Since when did any *normal* cat like to swim? There's more than a little bit wrong with Jeremiah. One day he climbs down the tree into our yard and sits by the pool, sunning himself for a full hour before going to the toilet, in the pool, and *then* having a swim.

I watch the whole thing.

As Jeremiah swims, I go to the garden shed. He circles his floating faeces like he's training for water ballet. I take bits of old chicken wire and fashion them into a funnel-shaped net. I attach it to the end of an old broomstick. I sneak out of the shed and watch Jeremiah swim. His mottled tabby fur looks darker, tea-stained from the pool water. I stalk him from behind and slam the net down over him. Jeremiah remains nonchalant and continues to swim.

'Got you!' I say, giving Jeremiah a look that might well have stopped a lesser animal's heart from beating.

'Now what?' Jeremiah says, not bothering to hide his disdain.

'I hadn't thought that far ahead,' I say before I realise I am talking to a cat. To a cat. 'Wait, you *talk*?'

'Don't you?' Jeremiah says.

'I don't like that sneer in your voice,' I say, as if I were speaking to a wayward child.

I squat down to look Jeremiah in the eye. I decide to try reason.

'Why do you defecate in my pool?'

'As good a place as any,' Jeremiah says.

'No, not really. Not at all. I can think of many better places. Like your own yard, for example.'

'Would you shit in your own yard?'

'Well...I...no I wouldn't,' I say. 'But, you *swim* in it after you do it, so what's your point?'

'My point is not about hygiene. You humans are all the same. You will never understand cat logic,' I swear I hear him sigh. 'Now, will you let me out of this ridiculous net? I can't swim for much longer, I'm getting tired.'

I see my opportunity. Clearly. I can just make him swim a bit longer and he will drown. He's an old cat. Nobody will question it. Everyone knows the cat swims in my pool. I feel murderous. Mad enough to do it. I push the net deeper into the water, making it harder for Jeremiah to come up to catch his breath.

'Can we come to an...arrangement?' he pants.

'No, no we can't. The time for arrangements passed when you defecated in my pool.'

'Are you sure, now? I can be very,' he splutters as he inhales a mouthful of pool water, '...helpful.'

Despite myself I am intrigued. 'What kind of arrangement? Helpful how?'

'Well. You know that woman Scarlett? She has a dog.'

'Well, sort of. She's not my kind of person, really.'

'Yes, no one likes her. She talks about you, you know. I would be doing the whole neighbourhood a favour, really, when you think about it. I could really tip her over the edge. You know, white jackets and padded walls, that kind of thing.'

'What do you mean, she talks about me?'

Jeremiah splutters some more, gasping for air as his legs slow to a near stop. He can't tread water any longer. I ease up on the net, allow him to stick his paws onto the broomstick so that he can rest and catch his breath.

'Thank you. That's terribly kind.'

'Well. Go on. What does she say about me?'

'She calls you crazy.'

'She does?'

'Yes, says you walk past her house talking to invisible people.'

'Well. Well.'

'So, let's give her something to really be concerned about.'

'Such as?'

'What if I, say, start having chats with her? She'll think *she's* gone mad, won't she? She'll stop calling you crazy!'

This gives me pause. '*I'm* standing here talking to you. You are talking back. That must make *me* the crazy one.'

Jeremiah realises his tactical error.

'I'm struggling here, can you let me out, please? We can keep talking on dry land. I'll explain. I think I'm over swimming pools anyway.'

'Let you out? Why, so you can go around telling people I'm the crazy women who talks to cats! I know your plan!'

I press harder on the broomstick, pushing Jeremiah under water. I have to lean in to push it deep enough, and that is my mistake. Jeremiah's claws are poking through the wire and he swipes at me, drawing blood on my forearm. I scream and pull my arm back. In a flash, he swims to the edge of the pool and uses my broomstick to crawl out, while I drip blood onto my pavers.

'You vile creature! And to think I was about to trust you!'

Jeremiah is breathing heavily. He shakes furiously, hisses at me, just like a regular cat might, and scoots up the tree and into his yard, as though the whole thing never happened.

'There you are, Jeremiah,' I hear Denise coo from over the fence. 'Why are you so wet? Come here, darling, let me dry you off.'

'He's been in my pool again, Denise!' I screech over the fence.

Denise pokes her head over the fence.

'Goodness, what happened to your arm, Marg?'

'*He* happened to my arm, Denise! Your cat scratched me as I was trying to *rescue* him from our pool!'

'Oh poor darling Jerry, are you okay?' Denise says to the dripping cat. 'Hope you've had your shots, Marg.'

I don't answer her because I'm already forming a plan. I wonder how many of Martin's EpiPen shots would be required to knock out an animal that weighs, oh, about eight-to-ten kilos.

MARTHA AND CHARLES

Gaps Between Boxes

Last week I tried to tell Charles all of this, but he wouldn't listen. I know it's hard for him to hear, but it has to be said. He wants to live here forever, just to keep it clean. He wants me to keep the garden neat and plant new pansies each spring. He'll trim the fruit trees and I'll nip the flower buds off the herbs to drag out their productivity. I'll mulch. He'll dig trenches for the rainwater tank drip feed to keep my flowers fresh in summer.

On Sunday nights we'll sit at the dining table and go through the bills, just like we've done since 1975. On Mondays I'll wake up and remember I don't have to go to work anymore and neither does he. I'll look at this house — this beautiful house — that we built together and made into a home and wonder what actually needs to be done.

Nothing. There is nothing left to be done. We ticked all the boxes.

So now are we supposed to hang up our desires and dreams and settle in with a cup of tea and the telly, passing each other the heart-smart margarine over our toast in the morning?

Charles has always wanted an easy life, but I never did. And now that easy life feels like meandering slowly towards death.

All those boxes we ticked, the house, the kids, the jobs. Whenever I ticked a box, I was wondering, 'what's in that gap, in between the boxes?' But how do you do the in between when you are on the path that we were on? A path laid out for us by our parents and their expectations, and the society we were raised in, and its expectations, which were one and the same because in those days people did what was expected of them: get married, buy a house, raise kids, retire silently, get sick and die. I remember telling Anna when she was fourteen to always question other people's expectations to see if they sat well with her expectations of herself. But I never took this advice myself.

Now I am taking it. No more regrets. No more pining for the gaps in between the boxes.

When we met, five-year-olds in preschool, Charles was an adventurer. In love with the idea of the Scarlet Pimpernel. He was the most exciting person I'd ever known. I think I fell in love with him then, even though it took me twenty years of friendship to realise it.

This has been a wonderful place to live and raise a family. But now it's a millstone. The garden that I cherished and tended to for decades now makes me angry when I look at it. I think of all the hours I spent in it instead of travelling the world. I walked the paths between the citrus trees when I could have been walking on cobblestones in Damascus. The floorboards that I have vacuumed more times than I've drunk champagne make me wild with a rage that scares me because I imagine all the railroad tracks I've never seen and the rattly carriages I've never sat in and all the windows I've not looked through onto blurry landscapes. The kitchen. Oh the kitchen. How many meals have I prepared in it? Let's work on averages. Forty years of marriage. 365 days in a year. Three meals a day. Four family members. I can't look at that splashback anymore without wanting to take a hammer to it, turning it into the mosaic of a Barcelona garden.

Will he come with me? I am leaving, with or without him. We can still have great adventures together. We can seek out the gaps between the boxes. We are not too old.

Dear Martha

I'm leaving this letter on the kitchen table because I can't face you right now and talk in a civil way.

Meander slowly to death? That's what you think I'm doing? I just don't want to fight, Martha. I want peace. Is that so bad?

I know you will sit down at the kitchen table tonight, even though I'm not there. Forgive me for putting the electric bill underneath, but it must be paid.

Don't worry. I haven't topped myself or taken off with another woman. I'm staying with Anna for a few weeks. I suppose you will be gone by the time I'm back, but I need to clear my head. Your talk of boxes and gaps has me feeling wretched. I can't begin to order the thoughts in my head.

All I can say with certainty right now, in this hour before I put the letter on the dining table and leave the house you now despise so much, is that I never looked between the boxes. For me the boxes made a darn good life. I have always been satisfied and it frightens me to learn now, after so many years together, that you were not satisfied, as I imagined you were. How could I not know? Why didn't you tell me?

Charles

So it seems we won't be taking this trip together. Stevo has booked me: Adelaide – Singapore – Dubai – Dubrovnik. It's one way. I will send enough postcards for Charles to repaper the hallway.

Dear Martha

I am writing to you care of the post office in Florence. I do hope you are still there, and still checking in for mail. Tell me when your email is up and running, it's driving me mad waiting so long between postcards.

The house has a buyer. They have offered the asking price. There are papers to be signed. The buyer wants a quick settlement. I fear that if I can't get papers to you in time the sale will fall through.

Please get in touch. Now that the sale is real, I am feeling quite relieved of it and want it done.

Charles

Dear Charles

I have opened an email account, although I have to admit I've enjoyed my trips to the post office enormously. They know me there and it is lovely. They tolerate my stunted Italian and compliment me on my postcard choices. Each time I visit they teach me a new word. Today it was *tramonto* which sounds much more poetic than 'sunset', don't you think? You must try to say it with the Italian flourish, not our flat Australian accent. It always sounds better if you use your hands.

Can you attach the papers to an email please? Get Anna to help.

Martha

Dear Martha

Anna laughed at my incompetence in scanning and attaching documents, but I'm learning new things. She's happy you are having fun and says to say *ciao*.

How is Florence? Have you seen Michelangelo's David yet? And the Ponte Vecchio? I've been reading up. It sounds wonderful. I would love to buy you a little gold pendant on the Ponte, a house on a chain. Do you think they sell such things?

Charles

Charles

You old fool. Go to the Flight Club on Goodwood Road. Ask to speak to Stevo. He has a ticket for you: Adelaide – Singapore – Rome. The train to Florence is a piece of cake. You only need a few words in Italian to get around here.

I've been strolling the Ponte Vecchio daily, looking for the pendant you describe. There is no kind of jewellery you can't buy on that miraculous little bridge. It's just a matter of finding the buried treasure. It's a wonder it doesn't collapse under the weight of all that gold.

With love and anticipation

Martha

Dear Martha

I went and saw Stevo (don't young people have normal names anymore?) and it was all arranged, just like you said. Even the train from Rome to Florence. You are a marvel.

Martha, I can't do this…flights, trains, passports, speaking Italian? I've told Stevo to put a hold on it all.

Keep looking on that bridge. I know you will find that pendant, in a little gap between the boxes somewhere.

With love

Charles

So Much Sand and So Much Water

The cliff is steep, crumbling ochre walls stretching from sand to sky. The old concrete steps are still there, clutching onto the cliff and overlayed with new wooden steps. Charles wondered if he could walk down those steps now, much less up them. But when he was a child, he would *run*. Surfers would stand aside, holding their boards out wide, as he sprinted, his parents puffing behind.

Charles hurried down to the beach.

'Hurrah!' he called to the sea. 'I am The Scarlet Pimpernel, you can't beat me!'

He hit the sand and didn't feel the heat of it on the soft flesh of his feet. He spotted the rock pool and ran in search of crabs. His battle cry could be heard up the beach and down.

Reaching the pools of warmed salty sea he conducted a thorough and exacting inspection, picking up rocks and putting them back down, disappointed that there was no sign of life. His search complete after several minutes, he looked impatiently back to the steps. He started jiggling and pacing and occasionally rechecking a rock here or there. There were no crabs; must be too late, or too hot. And when would she *get* here?

A small figure made its way carefully down the wooden steps, taking each one seriously as though she'd been warned too many times that she might fall. Clutching the handrail she got closer, a fluttering yellow shape turning into a ten-year-old girl. Charles wasn't looking, but someone pointed to him and she ran.

'Charles! Charles!'

Charles looked up and saw Martha.

'Ah-huh! I am The Scarlet Pimpernel! You may call me Sir Percy!'

He struck a pose, bracing his feet in the soppy sand, aiming an imagined sword at the sky.

Martha giggled and brushed some kicked-up sand off her dress.

Charles's weapon was suddenly forgotten and he looked at Martha properly.

'Would you like to search for lizards? There aren't any crabs here,' he kicked the water in the rock pool in disgust.

Martha's eyes popped.

'Lizards?'

'Yeah,' Charles grinned. 'I bet we can find a skink. Probably no monitors, though.'

Martha gave a little excited jump.

'Okay,' she said.

'Follow me! I know the way!'

Charles led her to the base of the concrete steps. He

wedged himself in a tight space between the rocks. Martha followed.

'Where are they?' she asked.

'They're here. You just have to be quiet so you don't scare them. Weapons away.' He tucked the imaginary sword into his shorts.

'Now, no talking and no fast movement. They live in little cracks and crevices where they can hide away from predators and if they hear you, they'll bury themselves so deep we'll never find them,' he whispered.

Charles inspected the cracks in the concrete, the places where the old structure was trying to break away. Martha looked too.

Old chip packets and tin cans were plentiful, but lizards were not.

Martha pulled her dress up to her knees and sat on her hands.

'I like it here,' she whispered dreamily. 'I wish...'.

Charles's mind stilled for a moment. A wish was a sacred thing, a thing he understood, a thing he respected.

'I wish we could stay here. Always. Live here.'

'Let's swear,' Charles said. 'Let's always come back here. Even when we are old.'

'I'm going to be a ballerina, you know.'

'And I'm going to be...something important. I just don't know what yet.'

Charles needed to get to the bottom of the cliff. His bones didn't want to get him there. But he had important business on that beach.

'Damn it,' he cursed as he took one step at a time, hips and knees cracking, one hand grasping the rail. People rushed past him, some knocking him carelessly, others giving him a wide berth. He was glad he hadn't asked Anna to come today. He couldn't stand her worrying about him. Finally, halfway down, someone stopped.

'Are you okay? Do you need any help?'

'Look that bad, do I?' Charles laughed.

The woman looked embarrassed.

'I'm sorry, it's just…it's a long way. Do you want me to carry that for you?' She pointed to the urn tucked under Charles's arm.

'Oh no, that wouldn't be right. Thank you dear, it's very kind. But I am on a mission, you see.'

'Okay, then,' she said and kept walking.

Step after step Charles made his way down until finally his feet reached the sand. He sat on the bottom step for a long time. Too long. He felt his legs cramping up, so he stood and walked to the sea. Charles slipped off his shoes and socks, rolled up his slacks and walked into the water, up to his ankles. The rock pool was still there, although it had been buried by sand over the years. The jagged rocks looked smaller than when he was a kid.

'Martha, my darling, this is for you.'

Charles opened the urn and tipped the ashes into the water of the rock pool. They swirled gently in the tide. Charles found a comfortable rock and settled in to wait for the tide to take her out to sea.

JENNIFER, ALEXANDER AND DAN

The Exhibition

I have a little exhibition of my paintings. Not a proper one with media and VIPs, it's just for friends and family. I have a dozen paintings hung on the walls of an old greengrocer's shop that's been converted into a gallery about the size of a pea: Mrs Ferris' Grocery Shop. The room is full with twenty people in it. We serve orange juice and vodka and put out bowls of roasted chickpeas and Kalamata olives. The paintings are okay, but nothing special. There are eleven horizons and one burrow. People look at them and smile and say encouraging things. My mother buys the smallest horizon. She'll hang it in the hallway where it's dark and the globe is never switched on because in two steps you are in another room anyway.

The stunning, svelte Alice from up the road buys a medium-sized horizon. The ponytailed man on her arm looks at her as though she is the answer to every question he ever asked. Maurice examines each piece carefully and with a gentle respect. He treats it like it's real art and I love him for it. Florence sits quietly on a chair looking forlorn and doesn't speak to a soul. Nothing else is sold. People hug me and leave after an hour. Dan takes Ava home so that I can tidy up, and soon enough there are only two people left in Mrs Ferris' Grocery Shop.

Act 2

Scene: Mrs Ferris' Grocery Shop, 81 Plane Tree Drive—night, now Jennifer locks the door and lowers the Venetian blinds, shutting out the street.

'I didn't know you painted,' Alexander says.

'I am a woman of myriad mystery,' Jennifer says with a wink.

'No you aren't, I know all your mysteries. Except for the painting.'

Jennifer remembers Alexander visiting her in hospital when she was twenty years old and grieving her baby all on her own and she knows he's right. He was there long after her son's father had bailed. He held her hand and cried with her. And then he vanished back into his world, as he did, leaving her to drift in her grief slowly towards a new life with Dan.

'Tell me about the burrow,' Alexander says.

'It kind of stands out, doesn't it?'

'Like dogs' balls.'

'Well, I went on a painting retreat and there were bloody trees everywhere. I'm sick of looking at trees.'

'So you found a burrow. What about a bird or a leaf or a person? Why a burrow?'

'I don't know. Have you ever tried to paint a bird? The

buggers won't sit still.'

Alexander laughs.

'Are you still making films?' he asks, taking a sip from his neat vodka.

'No, I'm making play doh.'

'That bad, eh?'

Something tries to rasp its way out of Jennifer's throat and she coughs it back. This exhibition was supposed to be her light.

Alexander cups her chin in his hand, looks her in the eye. 'You're lost.'

'I know,' is all she can say, but in a small way she hates Alexander for telling her the truth.

He rests his body against the wall, between horizons, and stares at the floor. 'When I was little, my grandparents were murdered by soldiers. Mum and Dad packed up me and Viktoria in the dead of night and we caught the first train – going anywhere. It took seven months altogether, but we ended up here, in Adelaide. Two weeks later, I was at school and you were teaching me English in the schoolyard.'

This is a story Jennifer's heard many times. She knows other details too – about the fear of those seven months, of the money running out and documents being stolen, about nights sleeping underneath his parents' bodies so he could remain hidden from child smugglers and thugs.

'Do you think your life has a point?' she asks.

'I used to think it did. Not so much now.'

'Why not?'

'Things haven't turned out...I don't know...*profound*. My parents used to tell us that we were lucky to be in Australia and we had to make the most of this new life. That we had been given a gift. Now look at us. Viktoria is working for the tax department and I'm designing shoeboxes that pass for public housing. There is nothing profound about our lives. Maybe we wasted the chance we were given.'

He looks so different now. Different to the way she sees him when she closes her eyes.

'Do you ever think about The Game?' she asks.

'Not for years.'

'I think about it all the time. How I hid behind it.'

'We both did. Why didn't we tell each other we loved each other then?'

How are they suddenly, easily, *finally* talking about this?

'I used to believe it when they said we were perfect for each other, except for *everything*. That *stupid* game. It feels like all those differences have been whittled away. Why did we think they were so important then?'

'That game used to shit me,' he says, but she's not thinking about The Game anymore. She's thinking about fixing this, because it all suddenly makes sense.

'We left our fingerprints on each other. All over. Outside and in.' She takes another deep breath and talks to the floor. 'I loved you so much it hurt. I loved you as much as any teenager ever loved anyone. Like Juliette loved Romeo,' she smiles at the melodrama of her words, but she remembers it so well. How it felt.

Alexander leans in, takes her face in his hands and kisses her on the lips. Her heart is careening in her chest as she tastes him for the first time and her entire life coalesces right there, amongst all the horizons with their cliff tops and sweeping winds and she can't stop kissing him. He tastes of twenty years of longing.

It's not awkward with bodies thrown up against walls and clothes torn off, it's quieter than that. They're ravenous but they are patient too, drawing out moments as long as they can, in case this is all they will ever have. She wants every touch to be imprinted on her skin so she slows everything down until the end, when it's impossible to be slow.

After

The waiter brings out the last plate of food to complete our banquet – a sticky plate of sweet, seared beef – and lights a small sparkler. He places it in Dan's rice bowl and gives a little bow.

'Happy birthday, Dan,' he says with a grin.

Dan forces a grin back, 'Another year bites the dust, Chen.'

'May you have many more, mate. Doing anything special this year?'

Dan spreads his hands out, indicating Ava and me. His smile is tight.

'Tomorrow I'm taking off for a weekend hike with some mates.'

'Well, have a good one.'

Chen makes a subtle exit and Dan, Ava and I are forced to look at each other again without the buffer of a near-stranger.

'The food looks good,' I say.

'As always,' Dan says.

Ava picks up a chopstick and pokes it in her rice, trying to imitate what she's seen us do countless times.

'You need two, darling,' Dan says. 'Like this.' He picks up Ava's other chopstick and places it in her hand, trying to rearrange fingers and sticks into the right places. Ava resists the strange feeling and gives up, throwing the chopsticks on the table and using her fingers to pick up individual grains of rice, fascinated by the texture on her fingers and tongue.

'We could be here all night at this rate,' Dan says.

I pick up my own chopsticks. I'm aware that I've ruined this and we will never do any of this again. No more birthday dinners at Lim's. No more sharing the small moments of Ava's development. There is no laughter tonight, that's all gone too.

Waiting until after Dan's birthday to tell him seemed like a good decision at the time, and having one last celebration together as a family, for Ava's sake, seemed like the right thing to do. But it's nothing more than diversion and denial. And Dan knows something is up.

Now, when I close my eyes in quiet moments I see Alexander and me at my exhibition. We are a movie I play back in my mind, and now I've got fresh footage. Making love with him did not erase him, it enhanced him. My imagination was low def, reality is high def.

'What are you thinking?' Dan's voice jolts me out of my memory. 'You were smiling.'

'Was I?'

'I remember your happy smile. It's been a while, but I'm pretty sure that's what I saw,' Dan says sadly.

I concentrate on my food because I feel dangerously close

to the edge of something irretrievable.

'You can tell me, Jennifer. I know, anyway. Don't think you are sparing me by waiting until this charade is over.' He waves his chopsticks over the embarrassingly laden table.

'You know what?'

'I know it's over. I know we're done.'

I glance at Ava. I don't want to have this conversation in front of her, in a restaurant, but maybe it's easier this way. No screaming scenes, no dramatics.

I can't look at him.

I finally raise my eyes to his and he nods. He shuffles his chair a little closer to Ava and makes a determined effort to ignore me while he helps her eat her food.

GARY, SARAH AND ABDUL

Car Park Job

Some joker has walked through seven floors of the car park and left flyers on every windscreen. The flyers, about the size of a wallet, are photocopied on the cheap. The writing is cut off at the top and bottom, but there is no mistaking the message: there's a phone number and a picture of a woman, hands scraping her blonde hair from her face, lips parted in phony ecstasy and breasts fairly bursting out of her triangle bikini. I have to take those bloody flyers off every windscreen before the car owners come back, or I'll have mothers screaming at me about mental scars. Makes me feel like a dirty old man just touching those photocopied breasts.

The car park is full, that means three hundred and fifty flyers. I'm about halfway there and I take a break – my fingers are tired from puckering the corner of the paper so that I can grab it and slip it out from under the wiper blade. RSI. I think about all the trees that had to die to make this pornography, and then I think about how that girl, whose face I've seen having the same sham orgasm a hundred times, is someone's daughter, some girl who grew up right – or maybe not – and then ended up doing this. Puckering her lips like some bloody gawping fish so that men can get off.

And then I think about my own daughter. Sarah hasn't spoken to me for six weeks. She's some big corporate deal and wears suits that cost more than I make in a month. Her shoes are peacock-coloured weapons, but she walks in them as if they are slippers. The last time we saw each other she sat across the table from me and pushed the mashed potato and sausages around on her plate like they were nuclear waste. She'd brought wine and drank more than she ate. When I told her she was too thin she said, 'Thanks.' When I grew up, being too thin meant that you couldn't afford to eat, now it means you have more money than God.

I take another break and look over the barricade to where the cars are banked up on the street below. It's a nice way to see the city, everyone on their way to something important.

I always think of Sarah when I lean out the window like this. She's in one of those big office blocks, somewhere out there. I go back to picking flyers off windscreens.

The boss showed us video footage of the flyer guy this morning, we're supposed to look out for him and tell him to piss off if we see him. He's skinny as a reed, dirty blonde hair, dressed in an old flannel shirt and those tracksuit pants with the stripes down the leg. It'd be my pleasure to tell the weasel to bugger off but I know he's not coming back, not today anyway.

Molly would have told him to bugger off, too. Never met a broad who loved a fight more than my Molly. I drove her mad with my attitude. She called me 'lackadaisical', she loved to use words like that – she would spend hours on the crosswords. I know she would have liked a husband who got fired up from time to time, but I was never gonna be that fella. Sarah never forgave me for Molly dying. You'd think it was me driving the car that hit her, the way little Sarah turned on me. Poor blighter, I was about as much use to her as a shovel without a handle.

I've stuffed all the flyers into the plastic bag now so I take my place in the booth. All this thinking about Sarah and Molly has made me melancholy and I want to pick up the phone and talk to my wife but I can't of course. No phones in heaven.

I call Sarah instead.

'Sarah Wilson speaking,' she says.

'Sarah, love, it's Dad.'

'Oh?'

'Just wonderin' how you are. Haven't heard from you in a while.'

'Is that a car? Are you at work?'

'Yeah, it's okay. Abdul will get this one, I've got my sign up. Just wanted to say hello.'

'I'm busy, Dad.'

'Okay, love. How about coming over for a fish meal next week?'

'I'm pretty busy, you know.'

'Okay,' I say.

'Well, bye then.'

'Wait!'

'Yes?'

'How's work?'

'Really, Dad? How's work? That's all you've got to say to me?'

'No, of course not, love. You know I'm not much of a talker.'

'And I'm busy, so…if you've got something to say?'

'No, no. You get back to it.'

I hear the line go dead. I say into the beeping phone, 'Your mother wouldn't like what you've become, Sarah. No time for family. Rude to your father. She'd be ashamed of you, and she'd tell you too.'

I try to imagine the impact of those words, if she'd heard them. I can't. I don't know her well enough.

'Thanks, Abdul,' I call over to the other booth. Abdul smiles and give me his 'no worries' wave as I take my sign down and open up the booth.

A woman drives up and hands me a flyer.

'This was on my car,' she said. 'It's disgusting, I might as well park on the street.'

'Sorry, ma'am. I tried to take them all down, must have missed one.'

I hold up the plastic bag to show her all the flyers I've collected and a tear in the plastic splits clean down the middle with the weight of it and the flyers, hundreds of them, get caught in the little fan in my booth and blow straight into the woman's car.

She screeches like she's been slapped in the face as the paper breasts and puffed-up lips settle on her face, lap and cleavage.

Before I can get out of my booth and around to her car,

Abdul is already there.

'So sorry, ma'am, let me help you,' he says.

I watch Abdul as he picks up the pictures, one by one, from around the woman in the car. He holds the paper carefully, as though each piece is precious, even though of course it's not.

Oma's Fruit Cake

You should be at work but you are on bereavement leave. There are presentations to be polished, charts to be analysed. In bed at 10am, you log on to your laptop.

↓

You stare at the frightening sight of the backlog of emails.

↓

Decide tea is needed.

↓

While the kettle boils you decide to:

↓

Cut a slice of leftover Christmas cake.

Pull weeds from the garden.

↓

Notice the sunshine. Decide it is the perfect time to plant new seeds.

↓

Fossick for old toilet rolls, potting mix and seed packets. Search high and low for missing gardening gloves. Decide to get your hands dirty.

↓

Push the seeds in (cucumber, bean, corn and capsicum), getting black dirt under your nails and in your cuticles. Examine your dirty hands and feel satisfied that they have done something real, unlike when you tap at the keys on your computer.

As you scrape the dirt from under your fingernails, remember being seven years old and receiving a metal nail file with a pointed tip from Oma at Christmas. It was the most grown up gift you'd ever received and you loved her for it.

Remember the strange way she loved you. Distantly, awkwardly. Without touch. Still, you knew it was love.

Wonder if you added enough brandy to the cake: Oma always sloshed extra in at the last moment and this year she wasn't there to slosh. This was the first year.

Inhale the brandy-laced fruit; reminding you of the smell of her sweltering apartment and the cake as it baked for four hours in the summer heat. As a child you had been given specific tasks (mix, sift, measure, chop, melt), each more difficult as you got older, until you were capable of the entire job. But you were never trusted with the entire job, until now.

Remember another smell, this one sanitary and filthy. The smell of old people, indignity and death.

Try to forget that smell. Fail.

Eat the cake in an attempt to block out the smell.

Fail.

Go to the garden. Snap a twig of rosemary and rub the woody leaves between your fingers. Inhale the spicy sweet aroma.

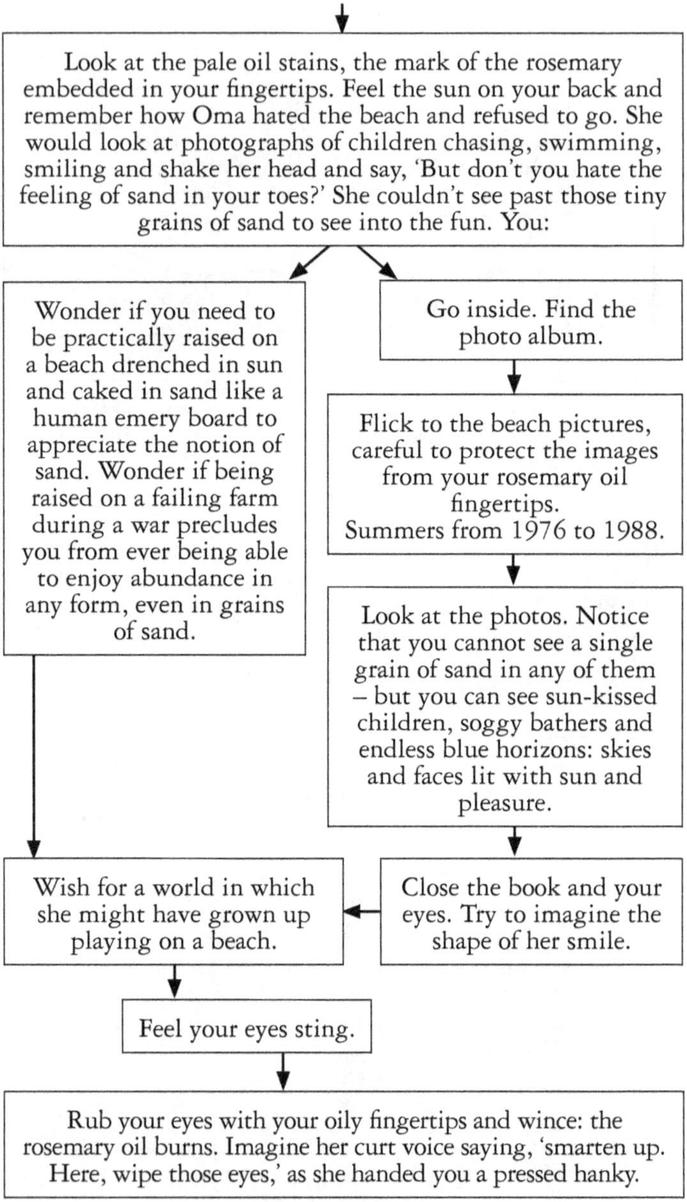

Look at the pale oil stains, the mark of the rosemary embedded in your fingertips. Feel the sun on your back and remember how Oma hated the beach and refused to go. She would look at photographs of children chasing, swimming, smiling and shake her head and say, 'But don't you hate the feeling of sand in your toes?' She couldn't see past those tiny grains of sand to see into the fun. You:

Wonder if you need to be practically raised on a beach drenched in sun and caked in sand like a human emery board to appreciate the notion of sand. Wonder if being raised on a failing farm during a war precludes you from ever being able to enjoy abundance in any form, even in grains of sand.

Go inside. Find the photo album.

Flick to the beach pictures, careful to protect the images from your rosemary oil fingertips.
Summers from 1976 to 1988.

Look at the photos. Notice that you cannot see a single grain of sand in any of them — but you can see sun-kissed children, soggy bathers and endless blue horizons: skies and faces lit with sun and pleasure.

Wish for a world in which she might have grown up playing on a beach.

Close the book and your eyes. Try to imagine the shape of her smile.

Feel your eyes sting.

Rub your eyes with your oily fingertips and wince: the rosemary oil burns. Imagine her curt voice saying, 'smarten up. Here, wipe those eyes,' as she handed you a pressed hanky.

DAN

Compartments and Venn Diagrams

In the library there are rows of carefully ordered books, in compartments assigned by Dewy.

My life is made up of compartments too.

In one, there is Jennifer.

In another, there is Ava.

Then there is me.

When we got married, I thought those compartments would join up somehow, that we would share our lives with each other. But the opposite happened. Jennifer buried herself in work, then in Ava, and I was on the sidelines. Mostly, I was happy to be there.

If our life together was a Venn diagram, it would look like this:

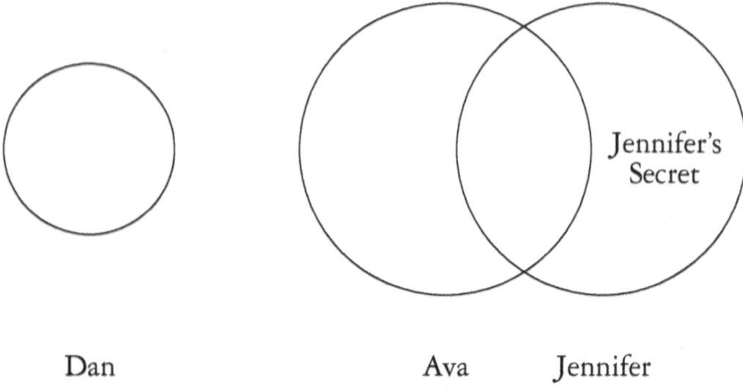

Jennifer's secret was never really a secret. I always knew she married me because I was solid, because I would never let her down. Not because she loved me.

The worst part about that diagram is the space between Ava and me. I know I can fix that, even if I can't fix anything else.

I wonder how it was possible that Jennifer once had the ability to break my heart. Now she is just a person I awkwardly share a house with, a person I am *entangled* with. We've been hanging on for so long that hanging on seems to be the whole game now.

The librarian gives me a bemused smile as she hands over the books Jennifer reserved for Ava, as well as the titles that are for us: *Surviving Divorce, Rebuilding After Divorce* and *Divorce Doesn't Have To Be Bad*. In a quiet corner I flick through that last one. The title seems improbable, but someone believed in it enough to write a whole book about it, so I'll give it a try.

One chapter is called, 'Two happy homes: how to help your children thrive through change'. I flick straight to that.

Ava seems like the most important part of all this. Whatever Jennifer and I inflict on each other will *not* be inflicted on Ava.

'The saying goes, children are happier in two happy homes than in one unhappy home. This is undoubtedly true. But change can be frightening for children, so it's always best to talk to them about what is happening. Explain the change in simple, unemotional terms and talk to them regularly. If you tell them once and then never mention it again, the whole subject of your divorce becomes a no-go zone. Talk often and talk honestly,' the author explains.

I flick to another chapter, 'Being friends with your ex: it *is* possible!' The cheerfulness of these titles irritates me. I wonder if it *is* possible for Jennifer and me. Were we ever friends to begin with? I plough on and read.

'What drew you to your ex in the first place? Perhaps a kind smile, a thoughtful compliment, or maybe it was that zap of electricity that we sometimes call 'falling in love'. Whatever it was, try and remember the positives...'

I slam the book shut. What a load of shit. None of this applies to me. The prospect of divorce doesn't scare me. I'm excited. I'm ready to start again.

I grab Ava's books and leave the divorce guides on the table.

The Swarm

We are a long way from Plane Tree Drive. No plane trees, just a forest of Casuarinas stands in front of us and the blazing moon tips over the apex of the highest tree. The others have gone to sleep. My muscles feel shredded and my thighs throb. I've ignored the blisters on my feet for too long.

I sit with him on the balcony smoking weed – the reward after the climb. We blow blue-grey smoke into the air and pass the small joint between us, careful to avoid touching, though as I place the damp roll of paper to my lips I'm aware that it's just come from him.

We talk about pointless crap – who was the fastest, who wimped out, who won't make it back – to avoid saying anything that might matter, and I drift off into thrilling and dangerous places. I want to leave everything behind. I don't want to protect my precarious and imperfect life anymore.

The joint is gone and I am joyous and hungry and pleasantly lightheaded. Now is the time, if there would ever be a time. I can say it's just because I'm high.

I stand, straighten my bulky jacket and wriggle my numb toes in their stiff, muddy boots. I stamp the mud off, ignoring my screaming blisters.

Well, we did it, I say. The summit. I keep my tone level.

He stands too. We don't hug as a rule, but the joint has freed us and hell, we just reached the top. We take a step towards each other with our arms half raised, eliminating the careful space we've always kept. I lean my body into him. We match, from our thighs through our hips, chests and to our cheeks. I take a breath, slowly in, feeling his body move with mine, and slowly out. I hold him longer than would be considered appropriate, but he holds me too.

He turns his head and I feel his breath flow over the exposed skin of my neck, carrying a soft humidity that hints of the tropics in this cold forest and spreads goose bumps down my shoulders. My skin puckers and bursts through the warmth of my thermals. This air expelled from deep within him arouses me beyond reason.

We do not let go.

The sweetness of the joint lingers in his hair and his arms are thick around me. I catalogue these things, file them into my memory, for later.

The time to end this moment has long passed, but I can feel his erection, throbbing against mine. Just when I think this is the most exciting sensation I've ever experienced, he presses his lips into the nape of my neck. He is hesitant, as though he's giving himself the option of calling it an accident. But my intake of breath is so sharp that he can't mistake my response. He continues. My eyes are closed against the forest and I push my cock harder against his. His kiss explores my ear lobe, finally reaching some electric place just below it and the question I had prepared and discarded, my complicated life and his responsibilities are all irrelevant. My thoughts are set free and feeling swarms into the moonlight. I can no longer summon any sensation of Jennifer's touch.

STELLA AND GRAHAM

North Atlantic Farewell

Graham

It is possible to be alive and dead at the same time. To live as though there is nothing left to be done, no work to conclude, no relationship to foster, no love to feel. It is possible to know that your death is so certain and so near that you are already in the throes of it. To be in the heart of death, to be living the pain of hell, to be absent to your loved ones, while your body obstinately withers.

For years Stella built walls, much higher and stronger than those in our home, so that when my day came she would be protected from her grief. I ignored this because it was more than I could bear. I blamed my fragile muscles, bones, nerves and tendons. But we realised that later the remorse for our lost days would come, so we chose a different path. The shadow of death will no longer be a companion, throbbing by my side. I will walk *to* death. My way.

My mind is claw-sharp. It has to be, otherwise I would not be deemed fit to make this decision. I have studied the brochure and watched the web videos and attended the mandatory counselling with sweet-faced Claudine.

My questions have been answered, all of them. Stella and I said our long goodbyes in the way that people who have been married for forty years can do. It took weeks and was sad and funny and felt like a gift.

Stella

Graham and I attended the *Final Destination's* christening. It made us feel like we were part of something bigger than just our pain. We watched Captain Mertens hand Queen Beatrice a bottle of champagne, which she cracked across the ship's monstrous hull and said in French, Flemish and English, 'May your travels be comfortable and your final destination glorious'. The ship was officially put into service and an hour later we boarded. Wheeling Graham around the ship we marvelled at the gilt sculptures in the atrium, the shopping mall with gifts of memorial photos, engraved pens and Belgian chocolate, and the peaceful spray of the neon-lit water feature. We sat down to our evening meal – the silverware stamped A835 in a barrel lozenge and the wine imported from all the right regions in Europe, Australia and the US – retiring to our cabin to sleep on 400 thread-count Egyptian cotton sheets.

As the sun rose the following day, the *Final Destination* encountered a protest vessel. The *Life Warrior* had apparently been following us since Zeebrugge. She sidled dangerously close and the protesters stood on deck with their posters, frowning at us shameful sinners. The two vessels, ours enormous and imposing, theirs small and pugnacious, cruised into the international waters of the North Atlantic Ocean, each watching the other with suspicion.

On the third day, the Captain of the *Life Warrior* took to the megaphone. 'So do not fear, for I am with you! Do not be dismayed, for I am your God! I will strengthen you and help you! I will sustain you and rescue you!'

Graham

These protestors continue to follow us and blast us with their monologues of death and doom. Don't they know that all of us have looked death in the eye, given it a teasing butterfly kiss to test how it reacts? We have questioned death more deeply than any of the truly living. We understand it and know it for what it is. It is hard for them to hurt us now.

Anyway, many of us are old and deaf.

Stella

The night before the burial, Captain Mertens addressed the ship over the PA. 'Thank you for entrusting us with your dignified burial. Tomorrow your suffering will end. It is important that you know that despite our attempts to outrun her, the *Life Warrior* continues to follow us. I have been informed that she is approximately thirty nautical miles from us now, and gaining. By the time we begin the ceremony tomorrow, I expect she will be alongside us again. Unfortunately, we have no power to have her removed from international waters. She is within her rights to be here. As are you. I remind you that you are not breaking any laws. As passengers on the *Final Destination* in international waters you are subject only to the laws of Belgium. I ask you to remain strong, one final time, and trust that we will protect you and undertake your final request with dignity.'

At the conclusion of the Captain's speech silence echoed through the ship. I imagined it to be like those moments as the *Titanic* sunk, as those clinging to her rails or scavenging from pockets of oxygen knew that a gulp of icy ocean was inevitable and they were powerless against it.

'Stella, can you take me to the foredeck, please?'

I wheeled Graham to the bow of the ship, set his brakes and sat down next to him on the polished oak seat, resting my hand on the brass rail. The sky was cloudless but Graham watched the water of the North Atlantic, today as dark as Indian ink.

I took my husband's hand. My weathered but pliable skin pressed against his fleshless bones. We sat on the foredeck long enough to see flying fish frolicking in the water below. The sun was starting to set and the air turning to chill when another boat appeared on the horizon.

'Let's go in,' I said.

By morning, all preparations had been made. The crew were efficient and precise, professional and sombre. A few passengers had changed their minds, as had been expected. But Graham was ready, as was I.

At our final counselling session Claudine spoke very little. I missed the sound of her voice – her English, with its lovely French lilt, reminded me of being in Paris with Graham on our honeymoon – and I wanted to hear more of it. But Claudine left an empty space for us to fill.

In the adjoining chamber, which held a large bed facing a

metre-wide porthole and a small array of medical equipment, the appointed doctor and nurse waited. We could have as much time with Claudine as we needed, but we were ready. We had said our long goodbyes and this morning there was not much we still needed to say. Throughout our married life we had been frank with each other and to both our amusement we discovered that the vast majority of the things we said over the years were positive.

'Telling each other any final thoughts is an important part of the process,' Claudine eventually advised.

Was there anything left to say? It seemed petty to drag up complaints now, but I trusted Claudine.

'I should have worked less. We should have had more holidays, like this *delightful* cruise,' Graham said.

Graham could always make me laugh, no matter how dire the situation.

We fell into silence.

After a while Claudine spoke. 'I'm satisfied that you are ready. Are you both satisfied also?'

Holding hands, we nodded.

Claudine signed the consent form, acknowledging Graham's fitness of mind and understanding of the consequences of the transaction. Graham and I signed our forms too, and I wheeled him into the adjoining room.

Graham

That she would do this for me, on top of everything else, is unimaginable. She will take me to the edge of life, holding my hand to ease my fears, leaving no room for her own fears to visit her. She will be brave. It is easy for me and so much harder for her, left with days, months and years to wonder and question and feel. I know she will ask herself if we did the right thing in the end. I look forward to not feeling a thing. My brain has been troubled by pain for so long that it is impossible to remember the lightness, the ease that comes with its absence. At the beginning of my disease I could blast myself into the background and be free enough, my eyeballs floating, my mind a jalopy and my body a jigsaw put back together by chemicals which took away my ability to finish sentences but locked away my pain. The soup of coloured capsules I swallowed day and night dissolved the infrastructure of my life and made it blissful enough for a while. Until they stopped working.

Afterwards, Stella will still have life to contend with, with no soup concoction to comfort her, not even my warm hand to hold.

Stella

I touched Graham's arm as he swallowed the liquid that prepared his stomach. I held his hand after his body was arranged on the bed. I grimaced with him as the needles were inserted into his lax and abused veins. I lay with him on the wide bed as the fluid was injected into the IV line.

We looked out at the ocean and spoke in whispers to each other as we waited.

I stayed with Graham for an hour after it was done, holding his hand tightly. After the tears stopped I studied my mind to see if it had been changed by this experience. Had Graham's passing, graceful and quiet in the end, proved anything?

Had there been angels waiting who turned him away? Was there anything left of him in this physical body that should be preserved in some other way? I could find no reason to believe in any of these things. I had farewelled my husband, the love of my life. He was gone. I would bear witness when his body, an empty vessel sewn tightly into weighted canvas, was delivered to the sea.

The burials began on schedule at fifteen-hundred hours. The crew, on this their first mission, appeared to function beyond the sum of their parts. The *Life Warrior* lay at anchor at a disrespectful distance, silently judging us.

As the crew brought the bodies to the burial deck, where families and crew were assembled in tight and dignified lines, the protestors on the *Life Warrior* held hands in a silent vigil of prayer.

Samuel Barber's *Adagio for Strings* played over the *Final Destination*'s PA.

I hugged my arms around my waist. The wind was shifting. The breeze had blown gently all morning, but now it was billowing in an unseasonal bluster from the north, blowing Barber's music over the *Final Destination* and the *Life Warrior* alike. The canvas-cocooned bodies slipped gently into the sea as the strings wove a warm nest around me and the wind whipped my hair into my eyes in an act of exuberant defiance.

Four Forgotten Objects

Packing up a house, more than anything, is an exercise in dust and grime. I've had to enter all those nooks and crannies I've avoided for years, the places where I've put things in order to forget about them. This dust is mostly made up of particles of skin left behind by me and my family. Microscopic reminders, genetic markers, proof of life.

Secondary to the immediate, tactile demands of this dirt is the more reflective experiment in letting go. I quickly discover the things I am capable of leaving behind. The empty space I create is slowly filled with a seeping ache. Without it, this thing made of plastic or wood, I am not quite myself. Things remind me that forgetting is impossible.

Back then I told people my name was Sandra, and even the teachers entered into this lie. Towards the end of high school my life appeared remade, but Sandra was window dressing. Shellacked like the tables and pianos Dad restored for a living. Time after time I'd watched as Dad ground down ridges with pumice and filled gaps with bees' wax before polishing over the top, but I polished over myself before the ridges and gaps had been filled. When I met Graham, all that changed. He wanted to know what was under the polish, what was in the valleys, the parts I had tried to pretend didn't exist.

June 1964: The Beatles are in town. I stuff my mother's work uniform and our best white towels into my school bag. Adelaide is powerless to defend itself against the mania. The police are taut, and my all-girls school is in the news: the gates are locked and there are threats of expulsion for any student who joins the mob in town. Headlines call it 'Adelaide's Prison School'.

I don't care if I get expelled. I'm in my leaving year so it makes no difference; my parents expect me to get a job in a shop. Jumping off the school bus, I wave goodbye to my friends and walk away from the school gates and into the city.

Pushing into the muscular knot of the crowd I am subsumed by bodies. The bracing and shoving, the firm hands of the police maintaining lines, the heels shaving ankles as girls and women jostle for position, the elbows and unladylike scowls, the enlarged, expectant eyes, the squeals and hysteria. I am indistinguishable amongst two hundred and fifty thousand people.

I get changed into my mother's cleaner's uniform in the John Martins dressing room and skulk around to the back entrance of the South Australian Hotel. No one notices me. I climb the service stairs and look into each hallway until I come to a busy and energised floor. I take the fresh white towels from my bag and make my way towards the room where the windows overlook the street.

'*Entschuldigen*,' I say, forgetting myself for a moment. 'Excuse me, please.'

They part without seeing me.

'Housekeeping!' I say, knocking on the door.

A man opens it and strides back to the window.

Standing in the doorway, my arms full of white towels, I take in every detail. The floral upholstered club chairs, bulbous yellow and brown lamp shades, strewn suitcases, empty tea cups. Everything seen through a haze of cigarette smoke. The unBeatleness of it all is breathtaking. A couple of men are chatting and looking out the window onto the madness below. There are no Beatles, there isn't even music playing. I don't know why, but I expected to hear 'Please Please Me'.

Finally, someone notices me.

'Hey, love, can I help ya?'

'I have fresh towels. Where should I leave them?'

'I'll take 'em.'

He walks over to me and tries to take the towels, but I tighten my grip and he figures me out.

'Alright, so, who'r you 'ere for, then?'

'What? I mean, pardon?'

'Which one o' them, eh? I can get you an autograph, if you don't make a fuss.'

'Fuss' sounds like 'fooss' with his accent and I can no longer speak. I nod like a maniac, my head bouncing up and down like I am trying to shake it loose. As I reach into my pocket to get the notebook and pen, the mood in the room shifts and the noise lowers to a hum. I know what this means: it is John.

' 'Ave you ever seen anything like it? Ever? It's like we're tossin' tenners out the window at the track! It's choss down there!'

Someone by the window, unaware of the holy presence in the room, has spoken loudly. A collective breath is drawn, as we all wait for John to respond. He doesn't. He ambles past them all, towards the door, towards me. He has something in his hand.

He looks me in the eye and I remember the seasick feeling I had on the boat to Australia. He takes the towels from my hands and passes me the thing he is holding: a shellac-covered cufflink.

'Can you see if they can fix this for me, love?' he says in that sing-song way he has and turns and walks away, carrying the towels, back to the adjoining room.

I close my hand around it, shut my eyes and tip my head back to the ceiling, thanking the god of rock'n'roll for this gift. With this one small thing I have solid proof of who I really am.

I am a Beatles fan.

Someone closes the door. I didn't get my signature, but I have an item that belonged to John Lennon. I study it. There is a chip in the shellac finish.

I watch the news with my parents. I don't tell them where I've been and when they ask about school I lie, making up stories about being one of the girls shaking my fists at the gate, demanding to be set free. My parents tut-tut and sigh, unable to understand having a fire in your belly for something so silly. When they were my age, their country was at war. I hope Mum doesn't notice the missing towels.

After dinner, I go out to Dad's workshop and turn on the light. I fiddle with his brushes and tins, smell the metho, benzyl and turps that he uses so frequently that they have become his aura – there is nothing of skin and sweat in his smell, it is all ethanol and turps, whether he is in the workshop or not. His fingers and the rims of his fingernails are the deep red brown of Australian Jarrah, so profoundly stained that the colour never comes out, no matter how much he scrubs.

I run my hand over the old, soft fabric of the drop sheets he uses to protect finished furniture. I slide my hand under the sheet and along the exquisite surface of a table top: the gloss is fine, feather-like: my hand is gliding on a warm film of ice.

I take the cufflink out of my pocket. Dad could make it good as new. Better.

There is a soft knock on the door.

'*Darf Ich hereinkommen?*' Dad asks, even though I am in *his* workshop.

'*Ja,*' I say.

He comes in and swaps to English, a sign that he is pleased with me.

'Vat are you doing out here, Stella?'

'Just thinking.'

He sees the cufflink in my hand and takes it, inspects it, turns it over, runs his fingertips over every surface. Somehow his fingertips are simultaneously coarse and smooth; veined with deep calloused cracks and polished with Jarrah.

'Very bad vorkmanship. No vonder it's *kaputt*. Who gave this to you?'

'Oh, I just found it,' I lie. Lies are so easy now.

'I can fix it, you vant me to? It could look very nice. Ve can make the colour better, even. Do you have the other one?'

'No, I don't. I don't want it fixed, it's okay.'

He gives it back.

'I vould never make something so poor. They should be ashamed, selling such rubbish.'

He rolls the 'r' in rubbish to show his contempt.

I tighten my grip on the cufflink until I can feel its imprint in the fleshy part of my palm, and kiss Dad on the cheek.

'*Gute Nacht*, Dad,' I say as I walk back to the house.

In my room, I pull out a small box that I have secreted under my bed. It was one of the few things we brought from Germany, and like everything else we brought with us — accents, history and shame — I have hidden it. I wipe the dust away from the wooden carving on top: stained red, yellow and black, the flowers are absurdly nationalistic. Inside are the treasures I'd been unable to leave behind. A small doll with raggedy hair and a palm-sized leather money pouch with a few silver Reichsmark. The coins feel hot in my hand, like they hold the fire of evil right there on those embossed swastikas and eagles. I put the coins back in the pouch and lay the cufflink next to them. I pick up the doll; her tangled hair catches on my broken fingernail. I smooth her hair in long slow strokes.

The next day at school my friends want to know whether my crazy plan worked. I tell them about John Lennon taking the towels from my hands, from my very own hands. They don't believe me, of course. Who would? But despite their accusations of bald-faced lies, I'm not tempted to tell them about the cufflink, not even for a moment.

Without Graham, the Plane Tree Drive house is too big and old. It's taken weeks to pack up our lives. The only room left to tackle now is the storage room, where I find these things, forgotten for over fifty years. The small wooden box, the doll, the silver coins and John Lennon's shellac cuff link.

I wonder at how, for so long, I needed these items, and then forgot them suddenly. But holding the Reichsmark I remember that keeping it was a kind of mental self-flagellation. By contrast, the doll confirmed that I was a child, I had not been responsible, I had not even been born. These two items – the coin and the doll – cancelled each other out. The wooden box, which was beautiful with its intricate carving and bold nationalistic flair, allowed me to see some good in my heritage, if I could just look past the shame. The box tipped the scale.

And the cuff link, well there was nothing complex about that: I was a Beatles fan.

I stopped stockpiling objects soon after that day I met Lennon, although I suppose this house is a collected thing, as well as a repository of all the other collected things. Family, vases, sheets, coffee cups, photos, stains and cracks have all been collected inside these walls. And now I have to distil all these things down to three rooms' worth so that I can fit in the unit. What would Lennon say, if he hadn't been killed that day? Something about my attachment to possessions? Maybe. But I like to think he'd understand.

JENNIFER AND ALEXANDER

Tea Cups

I buy odd tea cups in second hand stores – lonely items, strays that have lost their kind. I specialise in cups that appear to have been made in pottery class and discarded. These odd items, almost always brown, are beautiful. I look at them and see learning and imperfection and the flaws that are left behind by these things, like lines on a face, scars on a forearm, mended hearts, bulging veins, grey hairs. These things are beautiful. When I see a young face that has not formed its character through imperfection, or a body that shows no signs of life I feel no envy because I know that those things are yet to be. The time will come that those young bodies, perfect and strong, will fade and scar and flop, and I hope that the people inside those bodies will never be happier than when they are old.

I'm alive now. I look in the mirror and I see a person who has been brave for the first time in ages. I came clean with Dan. The time will come when I have to come clean with Ava too, but for now she is content.

I replay my last meeting with Alexander in my mind, another of the many movies I have of him.

Act 3

Scene: A coffee shop – day, 2 days ago

Ava sleeps in her stroller. A cup of tea sits in front of Jennifer, going cold. Opposite sits Alexander, calmly sipping his espresso shot.

The two are leaning in, minimising the space between them. Fingers near to grazing.

Jennifer rallies herself with the speech she has been planning for weeks.

'Alexander, Dan and I have come to an agreement. He's moving out. It will just be Ava and me in the house.'

Jennifer pauses, tries to gauge Alexander's reaction. He is impassive. Stony. Unreadable. He doesn't respond and too much time passes.

Jennifer is becoming agitated, rocking in her chair, afraid her emotion will wake Ava and she will cry before she has the chance to really explain. But she can't remember any of the speech she'd practised.

'Alexander, for God's sake, say something. Please.'

Alexander takes a sip from his espresso and places it on the table. Then he finally says something.

'Do you remember what you did when people called me names in primary school? You stamped your feet and told them off. They slunk away in shame. That's what you did – you made me feel like I had a friend. You were brave. You are brave.'

Jennifer remembers herself then, a ten-year-old version

of herself stomping her feet and standing up for what she believed in. Standing up against the bullies. That was before she forgot how to be herself, before she forgot she was capable. Before she believed those subtle, insidious messages about being a good girl, not causing a fuss.

Jennifer stands up, leans over and kisses Alexander on the lips.

'Thank you.'

'What for?'

'For reminding me who I can be.'

Alexander stands, and kisses her back.

It's About Time

Act 4

Scene: Alexander's kitchen – night, now

Jennifer and Alexander are kissing. Their hands grasp and graze each other's bodies, their lips locked, noses squashed flat. Wine glasses, full, stand on the bench. No music plays.

Jennifer stops, pulls back, and takes Alexander's face in her hands. She stares at him from a slight distance and holds his gaze. Alexander breaks into a smile first and Jennifer follows.

'We're really doing this, aren't we?' Alexander asks her.

'We really are.'

Fade out.

Fade in.

Jennifer and Alexander have moved to the couch, slightly less clothed.

Fade out.

Fade in.

Jennifer and Alexander are naked, hungry for each other.

Fade out.

Fade in.

Jennifer and Alexander are wrapped up, limb over limb, on the couch, their breathing beginning to slow. The wine glasses are still forgotten on the kitchen bench.

'We are becoming a habit.'

'A good habit,' Jennifer says.

'It's about time, don't you think?'

'We've wasted so many years.'

'Not wasted. We weren't ready.' Alexander says.

Alexander sits up straight, looking Jennifer in the eye. 'So what happens now?'

'We stop wasting time. We spend the rest of our lives together. I make you safe and you make me brave.'

'I like the sound of that.'

Jennifer kisses Alexander softly on the mouth. She rests her head on his chest and closes her eyes.

MAURICE, AMILY AND FARAJ (FEATURING THE SHED DOGS)

Sunlight Slippery Dip

He breathes little pieces of his insides into the world and says 'it's better to feel pain than nothing at all'. He has conviction on his side, but we are only nineteen. His voice reminds me of sitting around a campfire: someone has a harmonica, there is smoke in his words.

We lie under the full sized billiard table in his parents' house, at the good end of the Drive, the opposite end to where my dad lives. If he knew I was so close and didn't come and visit…well. Right now, sounds come from brown, rectangular speakers that are covered in something resembling hessian. I don't understand how the vibrations make it through that ugly surface unscathed. Light rolls through high windows, causing dust motes to dance and flicker. A single beam slides over the top of the record player and to the carpet below.

It's eleven in the morning. Anthropology text books lie discarded in the shadow of the sunlight slippery dip.

We are talking about what we would study if we were anthropologists. He is decisive in the way that he can be. Rock'n'roll, he says. Indie acts. He wants to get under their skin. He is exasperated by his lack of skill on guitar and wants to get to the bottom of it. What do they have that he doesn't? I feel like I could tell him, after all I grew up in the shadow of my dad's rock'n'roll haze. And it wasn't so cool. Or even interesting. All any kid wants is to be loved, or even noticed, by their parents. But it was all just fighting and resentment. I don't want him to know that about me. It will make him like me more, and for all the wrong reasons. Then he will want to meet my dad. The famous Maurice. And he will find out he's just down the road, but that he now works for a *bank* and he, this boy, will be lost to me forever.

I am not as decisive about what I would study if I was an anthropologist. I feel him pushing me to commit to something, to choose a path. But I can't. The world is big. How do you choose?

Now he is exasperated with me. He breathes no words; it's something I feel coming from him like a force field.

I stare at the underside of the billiard table – a huge slab of slate that is roughly hewn on the side no one is supposed to see – and wonder what would remain of me if it was to fall. What trace would I leave? I haven't done anything yet.

I stretch my hand up 'til my fingertips reach the cold rock. Undulations, ribs left over by tools pushing against the resistance of stone. I fall out of my body, becoming smaller as I sink through the nothingness of air into something unseen. I don't land. I just leave myself, disorientated as my fingers seek the slate, which is now too far away to touch.

I can't answer his question or have his conviction about anthropology or anything else. I'd rather life wash over me than take a stranglehold on it.

The Doors spin around the turntable and I still want to kiss him, even though he makes me feel as though I've lost my grip on myself. This thought is dizzying and I swirl until his smoky voice brings me back.

'If the doors of perception were cleansed everything would appear to man as it is, infinite,' he quotes Jim Morrison, who quoted Aldous Huxley, who quoted William Blake. I wonder if Blake was quoting anyone, or if this idea originated with him. Either way, Blake left the first trace.

He leans over and kisses me and I'm falling again, and it's not all that different to before.

An Opera in My Shed

The gigs didn't dry up until my skin did and now I enter payroll data for a bank. I sit in my fluoro-lit cubbyhole and tap at keys instead of sitting in the ink of a dimly lit stage, thumping skins. Instead of punters lining up outside the bar waiting to pay their entry fee and get stamped, each fortnight I have a small line-up of folks at my desk, irritable because I've typed one wrong digit and they have been underpaid. No one ever turns up to say they have been *overpaid*. Or to say, 'thanks, I was *correctly* paid'.

When Jacqui left, taking Amily with her, I dusted the remnants of them out of the house she'd always hated and my life by doing a reno job on my back shed. My shed is big. Corrugated iron. I put triple thick egg cartons on the walls, had a sparky come and put in a heavy duty electrical supply. I brought in recording equipment and amplifiers and put padlocks on the heavy pull-down door. I chucked all my tools and accumulated shit onto the back lawn, leaving it to rust, and now I have a studio big enough to be a small bar.

I dragged an old lounge in and pushed it against the wall, and in the back corner I plugged in a bar fridge. I fashioned a makeshift stage by putting down cheap shag pile rugs from IKEA.

Then I put an ad in Derringers:

Drummer seeking singer, lead guitarist and bass player for tribute band.

Some clueless kids called, asking what the pay would be. Some classically trained conservatorium graduates called and balked the second I told them what they would be playing – and where they'd be playing it. But then a few calls came through that seemed to make sense. Rowena asked, 'Do you have a rehearsal space because it can't be at my place, I have a baby. Oh, and is it okay that I have a baby?' I told her that babies were kind of essential to the human race and it was perfectly fine that she had one. David said, 'How many times a week will we practice?' He was disappointed when I told him only once. Miranda said, 'Is it okay that I don't know the whole catalogue yet?' It was the *yet* that won my heart. And finally, Dalton called. He said, with a tremor in his voice, 'I get performance anxiety in front of an audience. Is that okay?' I asked him if he could sing to me on the phone and when I heard him I decided it was my duty to help him. I'd seen plenty of other musos get over performance anxiety. And the world needed to hear that voice.

I invited them all – Rowena the Mum, David the Obsessive Rehearser, Miranda of the *Yet* and Dalton with Performance Anxiety – to my shed.

Dalton arrived first, anxious to check the levels on his mic in an empty room. He stared at his thongs while he spoke to me and while he sang. David and Miranda arrived together, all sly smiles, flushed cheeks and linked pinky fingers – they knew each other. Rowena was late. She rushed into the shed, out of breath and frazzled.

'Hi everyone. Sorry I'm late. Thing is, I have to put her down myself, she won't do it for Mum, and that takes forever because she is so slow on the bottle, and then she needs to burp – if I put her down without a decent burp she's *always* gonna wake up crying – and I have to stay with her and sing her a lullaby while I pat her...it's...and of course tonight of *all* nights, she just wouldn't go down. It's not always like this, I promise.' I think she said all this without taking a breath. 'Oh, I'm Rowena by the way. You can call me Row. Or Rowey. Either really, either is fine.'

I shut the shed door and we plugged in.

The sound from our rehearsal went straight through the egg cartons and the corrugated iron. I knew this because the neighbours complained. From one end of Plane Tree Drive to the other. That's when I remembered some advice I'd been given as a young man: if you're having a party, invite the neighbours so they don't call the cops.

We christened ourselves Maurice and the Shed Dogs and did a letterbox drop with flyers advertising a gig in my shed the following Saturday night. Some of the neighbours knew me by name and reputation, so I hoped the novelty of seeing an old has-been in action might bring in a few stragglers.

On Saturday night Dalton was nervous.

'Maurice, I don't think I can do this. I only came along

because I thought it would be just us, in the shed. I don't think I can perform in front of a crowd.'

'Man, you can sing the pants off these tracks. Just close your eyes and pretend you are singing down the phone to me again. No one else in the room.'

Rowena was tuning her guitar and eavesdropping on our conversation. I could see her bursting with the desire to add something.

'Dontcha think so, Row?' I said.

'Yep, he's the real deal, Maurice.'

'Better than the original,' I added, perhaps laying it on a bit thick. 'Well, I can say that,' I said, defending myself, 'seeing I *am* one of the originals.'

Rowena looked carefully at Dalton, dropping her gaze just before his eyes caught hers. Oh God, I thought, they're falling in love. In my shed. Now there's two of them – Miranda and David were like a couple of lovesick puppies, and now Dalton and Rowena too. Quickest way to destroy a band, in my experience, was for the band members to fall in love.

My work week at the bank seemed to fly by with the anticipation of Saturday night. As I sat at my desk inputting data I would think about the set list – was the order right? Was it the right mix of slow and up tempo? What worried me most was whether Dalton would hold it together. I could see him doing a no-show.

Saturday night came around and a few lonely souls drifted into the shed and sat on the couch. There was Jennifer, with Ava dozing soundly in her stroller. She was with someone new, not Dan, and they held each other close and whispered quietly into each other's ears. Young love that looked old. There was frail Florence from number 90; she must have left Doug at home, probably realising that the old jazz dog wouldn't like our relatively new school rock'n'roll material. And Alice, without that good-for-nothing ex-husband of hers, Tim. She had some hippie with her.

As per my instructions on the flyer, they'd brought their own booze and some had brought a packet of chips. I handed out old bamboo bowls, pointed them to the bar fridge and we were ready to go.

As the band tuned their instruments one last nervous time, I looked around for Dalton, but he was nowhere to be seen. Then I heard him: vomiting in the yard behind the shed. Not the greatest start – everyone else probably heard him too. But to his credit, he walked in and started to sing. He was looking at his shoes and his voice was barely projecting beyond the mike stand, but he was there and he was singing in front of real live people. This was not nothing.

After the first song he turned to me with terror in his eyes, looking ready to throw up again. Poor kid had no idea how good he could be if he just got over himself. I could see the meagre audience were fidgety and bored. He was not connecting. I looked at Row and Dalton followed my gaze. Bless her, she winked at him and blew him a shy kiss. He gave her a tiny nod and he looked at the crowd. Judging by their faces, he still had that same look of terror in his eyes. He was scaring the crap out of them. But he started to sing again.

The next song was pretty upbeat. From the early days of the band, before the singer became maudlin and melancholy, and before the drummer – that's me – had had an affair with the guitarist. Dalton *had* to sing that song with a smile on his face.

The advantage of being on drums is that you have a birds' eye view of everything happening on stage, from behind of course. I could see Row was watching every move Dalton made. She was worried for him, for sure, but there was more to it than that. This wasn't about the success or failure of the gig or even the band. The tilt of her head told me everything.

Dalton was managing to stuff up the chirpy song. The neighbours were getting restless. Something had to be done, but I had no idea what.

Row knew it too. She stepped up to Dalton's mic, locked eyes with him, forcing him to lift his gaze from the floor where it had once again slipped, and started to sing. Damn, who knew she could sing? She sounded like an angel. I think Dalton's shock took him out of himself for a moment and he actually started to sing too. For real. To her, of course. It was only to her. He still wasn't looking at the audience, but he was finally singing for real. It was like she'd just told him she loved him.

The audience felt it too. They stopped talking to each other and nibbling chips and started really listening.

And then it was there; that old feeling. The high of the gig-going-right. The symbiosis of five people playing together, getting each other, tapping into something bigger than the individual, feeling it, taking it beyond the notes on the page. It was all there. All because Row had told Dalton that she loved him. With a song. God, I love music.

The gig flew by after that and I felt like I was lost in

something easy and beautiful. The feeling that I only ever had on stage, that I'd been missing for years now, hiding behind that desk in that cubbyhole cubicle. I never wanted it to end.

But of course it did.

At midnight I waved the neighbours goodbye. Some asked if we were putting on a show next week, and that's how Saturday Night with Maurice and the Shed Dogs became a regular gig.

Saturday Night and Sunday Morning

More neighbours appeared the next week. Grouchy Marg who seemed to be talking to a roaming neighbourhood cat. That old fella Hal who'd hardly left his house since his wife died – he'd forgotten to change out of his pyjamas, but he was there. Jimmy was chatting to Hunni, both of them looking like awkward wallflowers.

They all brought something – a chair or an esky or a bag of chips. Saturday Night with Maurice and the Shed Dogs became a Plane Tree Drive institution – I knew this to be true and not just some flamboyant dream when the coffee van parked out front of my house one night, followed by a Burger Bar truck. They stayed for an hour, filled everyone with grease and caffeine and headed off. The now fifty or so people who rocked up to my shed were fuelled. Ready for the long haul. And the gigs did get longer, and longer, until we were still playing at three or four am, Dalton's voice cracking, Miranda's fingers bleeding and Row's breasts leaking.

Summer set in. The leaves began to change colour on the

plane trees as more and more people came and started to sit in my driveway, under the stars. The young hipsters came – the rich kids from the big houses at the top of the street, and the young ones from the flats at the bottom of the street. Chaining their commuter bikes to my cyclone-wire fence, they would squat over the gravel in their shorts and beanies and unshaven faces. The first followers – the older neighbours – graciously welcomed them to what had very early become their turf.

I loved seeing half my neighbourhood in my shed but the truth was that there were only two people I really wanted to come. Maybe I'd done this whole thing for them? I'd sent Amily and her mum a flyer. More than anything I wanted Amily to see this, to see her old dad almost like he was in his prime.

Months went by and neither of them came. I consoled myself with the growing audience of neighbours. I was left with nothing to do but make the best of what I had. And things were looking up. Dalton had become quite the entertainer. He coated the lyrics in treacle and made them romantic to the point of mawkishness. The reason Dalton sounded like caster sugar cut with white chocolate was that he was singing to Row. David and Miranda ogled each other with thinly veiled lust as the songs bore themselves out, David's licks on the bass getting quicker and quicker, pushing the pace of the song to its limits, as their blood pressures collectively rose. It was like watching a sexy soap opera in song every Saturday night in my shed.

After a few months I rang my ex-wife and asked her to come along with Amily one night. There was a lot of hurt in her voice when she said she'd think about it.

I rang Amily's mobile and begged her to convince her mum to come, or to come alone if her mum refused. Amily sounded torn. Poor girl was between a rock and a hard place, and her mum and I had put her there.

Week by week the audience grew. The neighbours brought along their friends, who brought along their friends and their dogs. One night I saw Marg talking to a Labrador, looking for all the world like she was having an in-depth conversation with the animal.

Four months into the shows a skinny, dark-skinned boy turned up looking lost and dirty. He squatted in a corner and didn't speak to a soul. At the end of the night he snuck away and I was mad at myself for not saying hello. I hoped he would turn up the next week, but he didn't.

One night as the leaves on the plane trees were starting to fall, and Amily and Jacqui still hadn't come, the dark-skinned boy came back. He sat in the same corner, squashed up against the egg cartons, fiddled with the hem on his ragged shirt and didn't speak to a soul. But I saw him tapping his foot.

After the gig I walked straight up to him, not wanting to risk him running out on me again.

'I'm Maurice,' I said, holding out my hand.

'Faraj,' he said, and shook my hand in a way that made me wonder when he last ate.

'Do you live on the street?'

'Yes,' the boy said.

'Which number?'

'Number?'

'Which house do you live at?'

'Oh, no. Not in a house. On the street.'

The child looked like he would break in two under a soft breeze.

'Do you play?' I asked, pointing towards the makeshift stage.

'No,' he said wistfully.

'I can teach you, if you like.'

He didn't answer.

'Come back tomorrow morning. We can have some breakfast and I'll teach you some beats. D'you like the drums?'

Someone slapped me on the back to say goodbye and I turned away from Faraj for a moment, and just like that he slipped away.

The crowd thinned out slowly after that. It was a crisp autumn night before the real chill of winter and people were reluctant to leave the sweetness of the evening behind. The shed and driveway were strewn with paper coffee cups and crushed chips, the green IKEA shag pile carpet that Dalton stood on while he sang was sodden with beer. The shed was a mess, but it was my mess and I loved it. The only thing that was needed to make it feel like the pub in the old days was some lipstick-stained, Hep-A-contaminated beer glasses and smoky lighting. Maybe I should invest in some better lights, I thought, as I waved goodbye to the last of the stragglers.

I was about to pull down the stiff shed door when a figure walked towards me from the street. Even though she was only a silhouette, I could tell from her walk it was Amily.

'Hi, Dad,' she said.

'I didn't know you were here! It's great to see you.' I

reached out my arms and she hugged me awkwardly.

'Well, there were about five million people here tonight. I'm not surprised you didn't see me.'

'It was a big night.'

Amily inspected the shed.

'I like what you've done to the place,' she said with a twist in her voice.

I couldn't help myself.

'*I* liked it better with you and your mum here.'

Amily didn't answer. I should have kept my stupid mouth shut, not dragged her into my messed up head again. She walked over to my kit and sat down. A rush of memories hit me: Amily aged two, bashing my kit for the first time, the cymbals her favourite noise; Amily aged six on her own miniature kit, her face serious with effort, tongue curled out of the corner of her mouth, trying to remember the rhythm I was teaching her; Amily aged twelve, headphones on. By then she'd given up on making music and only listened to it.

Now, she picked up the sticks and tentatively tapped the skin on the snare. The child had no rhythm, but she hardly needed to inherit my only skill.

I resisted the urge to correct her hold on the stick and tap my foot like an instructive metronome. I just waited for her, watched her tinker.

'How's your mum?' I asked.

'Happy,' she said.

The word hit me like a road train. Happy.

'So am I,' I said, and it was true.

'I can tell,' she said.

'And you, darlin'? How're you?'

Amily shrugged. A teenager's response. 'I'm okay.' She stood up, leaving the sticks on the snare and wandered around the room, touching things here and there, inspecting my new life with the lazy nonchalance teenagers were supposed to exude. I sat down in her place and started tapping out a soft beat, giving the gaping silence between us a backdrop.

'Can I make you a cuppa?' I eventually asked her. What I really wanted to say was, 'Darlin' I miss you like hell, come home.' But I didn't.

She nodded and we walked into the house.

'You haven't made the house into a pub or anything, have you?' she joked, the first real Amily smile I'd seen in far too long.

The next day I woke up first and put on the kettle. I left Amily to sleep in her old room, unchanged since she and her mother left.

As the kettle boiled I heard a soft tap on the front door.

Faraj.

I'd forgotten my promise to make the boy breakfast and teach him to play.

'Faraj, come in! Come in!'

I ushered him into the kitchen and motioned for him to sit.

'Cornflakes okay?' I asked. There wasn't any other option. Fortunately he nodded.

I put a bowl in front of him and he ate slowly. I could tell he was starving.

I filled his bowl up for the second time, and Amily emerged from her room, hair a mess and still in last night's clothes.

'Morning, love,' I said. 'This is Faraj. He lives on the street.'

'Hi, Faraj,' she said sleepily.

Amily filled up a bowl of cereal.

'Faraj, you want to learn some beats?'

The boy nodded and stood up with the barest hint of a smile.

I looked at these two children in my kitchen and I thought; this old fella still has a few good years in him yet.

'Come out to the shed when you're done, Ams?'

I ruffled her birds nest hair and she nodded as I led Faraj to the drum kit.

'You got rhythm, Faraj?' I asked him.

'I don't know, Maurice.'

'Anyone in your family play?'

He didn't answer so I looked at him. His brown eyes were glassy.

'Only soccer.'

'Ah well, there's hope for you yet, son.'

THANK YOU

It takes a village to write a book. I may have been the one at the keyboard, but there were many others who were with me every step of the way, and those who were there at various – critical – points.

Thank you to the publications who accepted some of these stories. I don't have words for how important it was to me to have those first few stories accepted. Having a few 'okay, I can do this' moments along the way gave me the courage and conviction to continue.

Ryan O'Neill generously ceded to my near-begging to be my mentor. I knew you were the man for the job! Your gentle but astute feedback and insights elevated my work. Thank you for letting me dance in your shadow.

Ryan O'Neill also wrote an endorsement that made my heart leap and flutter, as did the delightful Michelle Wright (I'll *always* wish we could have used your first response, Michelle!) and the super-supportive and kind Professor Donna Lee Brien. Thank you all for taking the time to read my work and put together your lovely words about it. It's an honour to have your names on the cover of my book.

Dr Rosslyn Prosser held my hand through many dark days as I wrote the thesis that bore the fruit that is this book. Ros, you always knew just the right thing to say. Thank you for lifting me and listening to me.

Thank you to the University of Adelaide and the Department of English and Creative Writing. If my life was a book, things would start getting interesting the day my acceptance into the PhD program came in the post. That was the turning point and the beginning of many wonderful adventures and friendships.

Joanne Knott is a talented botanical artist. Jo, your drawing of a plane tree leaf was precisely what I had hoped to have on the cover of my book. Thank you for your beautiful work.

Kim Lock is a joy and a pleasure to work with. Kim, your cover design perfectly enhanced the gorgeous image of Jo's leaf. Thank you. I hope to work with you on many more covers!

Zena Shapter went beyond the call to scramble together a gorgeous layout under challenging conditions. I'm indebted to you, Zena. I love what you did to make my words look like a real book.

Thank you to my writer's group colleagues: Kristin Martin, Tom di Santo, Elaine Cain, Alys Jackson, Louise Friebe, Michele Fairbairn and Nicola McGunnigle. Your support has been invaluable and your comments on the many drafts this book has been through have made it immeasurably better. You rock, and you are my rock(s). Thanks for being my people.

Anna Solding, Publishing Director at MidnightSun Publishing, is a woman of unmatched bravery, determination, energy and imagination. Thank you for taking on this strange little project and facilitating a dream that I have had since I was seven years old. You are a treasure and a dear friend.

This book took seven years to write. That's seven years of Mark, Ryan and Katy giving up their time with me so that I could follow this path and attempt to hold onto my sanity. And seven years of babysitting by my unfailingly supportive and always available parents, Ross and Hannelore Washington. Thank you all for giving me time and space, and for understanding what it means for me to be able to write.

ACKNOWLEDGEMENTS

The following stories have been previously published, some in slightly different versions:

'North Atlantic Farewell' was published in *Transnational Literature* Volume 6, Issue 2, May 2014.

'Lia and Amos' was published in *Breaking Beauty* ed Lynette Washington, MidnightSun Publishing, 2014.

'Gaps Between Boxes' was published in *Aspire Magazine* April/May 2014.

'How to Disappear Incompletely' was published in *SWAMP Writing* Issue 14 March 2014.

'Housing Needs Assessment' was published in *Tincture Journal* Issue 4 November 2013.

'The Swarm' was published in *Stoned Crows and Other Australian Icons* eds Julie Chevalier and Linda Godfrey, Spineless Wonders, 2012.

'Hermit Crabs' was published in *SWAMP Writing* Issue 12 March 2013.

ABOUT THE AUTHOR

Lynette Washington

Lynette Washington is a short story writer, editor and teacher of creative and professional writing. She holds a PhD in Creative Writing from the University of Adelaide. Her stories have been published widely and in 2014 she edited the story collection, *Breaking Beauty*. In 2017 she co-edited the story collection, *Crush*. *Plane Tree Drive* is her debut. When she is not writing, she teaches police cadets the importance of sentence structure and grammar.

Also available from MidnightSun Publishing

'The characters are treated with heartwarming tenderness ...

the Swedish settings vividly realized.'

J.M. Coetzee, Nobel Laureate in Literature

Nominated for six awards,

including the Commonwealth Book Prize.

MidnightSun

www.midnightsunpublishing.com

MidnightSun Publishing

We are a small, independent publisher based in Adelaide, South Australia. Since publishing our first novel, Anna Solding's *The Hum of Concrete* in 2012, MidnightSun has gone from strength to strength.

We create books that are beautifully produced, unusual, sexy, funny and poignant. Books that challenge, excite, enrage and overwhelm. When readers tell us they have lost themselves in our stories, we rejoice in a job well done.

MidnightSun Publishing aims to reach new readers every year by consistently publishing excellent books. Welcome to the family!

midnightsunpublishing.com

MidnightSun *Publishing Brilliance*

www.ingramcontent.com/pod-product-compliance
Lightning Source LLC
Chambersburg PA
CBHW020754190726
48285CB00006B/2031